THE LAST THING I REMEMBER

AN ABSOLUTELY ADDICTIVE PSYCHOLOGICAL THRILLER WITH A JAW-DROPPING TWIST

AF603763

KETAKI PATWARDHAN-NIRKHI

Copyright © Ketaki Patwardhan- Nirkhi
All Rights Reserved.

This book has been self-published with all reasonable efforts taken to make the material error-free by the author. No part of this book shall be used, reproduced in any manner whatsoever without written permission from the author, except in the case of brief quotations embodied in critical articles and reviews.

The Author of this book is solely responsible and liable for its content including but not limited to the views, representations, descriptions, statements, information, opinions and references ["Content"]. The Content of this book shall not constitute or be construed or deemed to reflect the opinion or expression of the Publisher or Editor. Neither the Publisher nor Editor endorse or approve the Content of this book or guarantee the reliability, accuracy or completeness of the Content published herein and do not make any representations or warranties of any kind, express or implied, including but not limited to the implied warranties of merchantability, fitness for a particular purpose. The Publisher and Editor shall not be liable whatsoever for any errors, omissions, whether such errors or omissions result from negligence, accident, or any other cause or claims for loss or damages of any kind, including without limitation, indirect or consequential loss or damage arising out of use, inability to use, or about the reliability, accuracy or sufficiency of the information contained in this book.

Made with ♥ on the Notion Press Platform
www.notionpress.com

To my family and friends, without whom I am nothing!
And to my readers, because of whom I can call myself an author!

Contents

Contents

Prologue

"She's moving her hand," somebody whispers.

The voice is unfamiliar, and it sounds like it is coming through a tunnel. I experience a slight twitch in my right hand before I lift it voluntarily. It is taking me a lot of effort to lift my hand and I can feel it. There are more muddled whispers. Some shuffling of clothes, some footsteps.

"Call the doctor," someone orders as I hear more noises around me. But I can't see anything. Everything is black. I try hard to pry my eyes open. They are open, yet all I can see is a dark blackness. Then suddenly out of the blue, a bright light penetrates that darkness, first in the right eye, then in the left. I involuntarily squeeze my eyelids shut, trying to resist that bright light.

"She's waking up," a deep masculine voice says with a tone of authority. "Inform Mr.Malik".

I

I am not sure what is going on. I am in a hospital, but I have absolutely no idea how I landed here. Ever since I opened my eyes, started seeing people around me, and attempted to move, I am being treated like a delicate glass doll that would shatter easily unless handled with care.

I tried to ask the nurse who was hovering over me, trying to make me comfortable but failing at it, but my throat still felt parched and all I could muster was a weird throaty sound that she ignored. It has been about an hour since I woke up, and I am waiting to see Nikhil. Where is he?

The door to my room opens and the doctor, the tall man with the deep masculine voice who had asked me a barrage of questions as I sat up, still confused and a bit disoriented when I first woke up, enters the room smiling.

I am about to ask him about Nikhil when he ushers a taller man inside.

This man looks like he has stepped directly off the ramp from Paris Fashion Week! With brownish black hair that adores his fair forehead, high cheekbones, chiseled jaw, and biceps that make their presence felt even from beneath the linen formals he is wearing, he looks like a model. No...a Greek God. But what makes me stare at him are his hazel brown eyes that bore into mine. He smiles slowly, and a dimple forms on his left cheek as he smiles.

Who is he? Do I know him? Is he a friend of Nikhil's?

"She is awake, finally," the doctor says to him, as he continues looking at me as if I am some successful experiment. "Over to you," he says, smiling at the man who wouldn't stop looking at me, his hazel brown eyes fixated on me, and leaves, leaving me in a complete lurch as to what to do with this stranger.

The Greek God continues to smile as he comes and sits on the chair next to my bed. I keep returning his stare, not knowing what else to do. Slowly, gently, he takes my hand in his and squeezes it. Suddenly, for a moment, I feel dizzy. This touch is familiar to me. I have felt it before. Shutting my eyes, I close them tightly.

"Are you okay?" the Greek God asks, worry lacing his tone. I open my eyes as I withdraw my hand from his grasp.

"Wh-who are you?" I stammer finally, after composing myself.

The smile suddenly vanishes from his face.

I keep looking at him for an answer. But he keeps looking back at me as various emotions flash across his face.

Disbelief, sadness, disappointment, disapproval?

"You don't recognize me?' he asks, his voice almost a croak.

I shake my head.

And suddenly, he gets up and he is gone.

What the hell? Why wouldn't he just tell me who he is and why he is here?

And where the hell is Nikhil??

II

"What is your name?" I look at the woman sitting opposite me.

She has tied her curly brown hair in a messy bun at the back of her neck. She looks at me atop her square wooden spectacles that have slowly slid down the slide of her perfect nose. She is wearing a diamond nose ring that shines beneath the bright lights of the room. Her neatly ironed white apron proudly displays her name tag, Dr. Riya.

"Mihika," I say, failing to understand the purpose of this exercise.

'Neurological assessment,' they have told me. Why, I don't understand. The Greek God has disappeared and no one would tell me where Nikhil is. They just look at me with pity, and irritation starts creeping inside me.

"Full name please," she says.

"Mihika Roy," I say.

She keeps looking at me. I can't tell what she is thinking. Am I failing at this test?

"What is the date today?" she asks.

"I don't know. I can't recall how I ended up here in the first place. I have no idea how long I have been knocked out. Under these circumstances, how do you expect me to know the date?" I ask, my anger slowly manifesting.

Dr Riya doesn't even blink.

"What year is this?" she asks, unfazed by my retaliation.

Now what kind of question is that?

"2017", I say, going along. The woman sits up straight, her pen abruptly falling on the notepad.

"2017?" she asks me in an incredulous tone, her eyebrows forming two perfect curves and her red lips forming a perfect O.

"Yes, why?" I ask, confused.

"What is the last thing you remember?" she questions, sitting forward, concentrating on the task at hand.

I screw my face in thought. What was the last thing I remember? Then it dawns on me. I can't remember the last thing I remember.

"I-I can't recall," I say, my voice trembling slightly.

"Do you remember the accident?" she asks.

"What accident?" I reply.

I have absolutely no memory of any accident.

Dr. Riya sighs.

"Where is Nikhil?" I ask.

If there has been an accident that I can't remember about, is it possible that Nikhil was involved too, and...he didn't make it?

Noooo.

That can't happen.

"Where is Nikhil?" I ask, more like beg her for an answer.

Her eyebrows scoot together. "Who is Nikhil?" she asks.

"My fiancé," I reply.

Dr. Riya waits for a beat before proceeding.

"When was the last time you met Nikhil?" she asks.

I try to think. I can't remember the last time. At all.

"I will tell you what I remember," I say.

"Okay," Dr. Riya encourages me to go ahead.

"So I and Nikhil live together on Pashan Road. I work as a manager at the Rounak advertising firm on MG Road and Nikhil works at Infosys," I tell her.

Dr.Riya looks confused, for a change.

"Which city are you talking about?" she asks.

"Pune," I reply, failing to understand the purpose of this seemingly fruitless interrogation.

Dr Riya gives me a look that I can't describe. Then she asks, "Do you know where we are right now? Which city?"

"Aren't we in Pune?" I ask slowly.

Dr. Riya shuffles the papers in her hand and gets up.

"Wait, please tell me what's going on," I plead.

Dr. Riya looks at me and something softens in her expression.

"We will tell you everything. It just has to come from the right person," she says and leaves.

*****

Every passing minute feels like a decade as I sit on my hospital bed, clueless, wondering what the hell is going on. My mind is a whirlwind of so many questions.

Why can't I remember how I came to be here?

Which accident was Dr.Riya referring to?

Why was she startled when I said this is 2017? Isn't it? Have I somehow time-travelled?

I laugh at the ridiculousness of my question. It would actually have been funny if it hadn't been so tragic.

Who is the Greek God and why was he here to see me?

Why did Dr. Riya ask me if I thought we were in Pune? If not Pune, where are we?

More importantly, what am I doing here?

And the most important question of all – where is Nikhil??

The door to my room opens slowly and the Greek God appears again. This time, he doesn't smile at me, but those hazel-brown eyes hold my stare.

I don't know what to expect. Should I smile? Should I frown?

He clears his throat as he takes a minute to steady himself, staring at the floor. Then he comes around my bed and gets seated on the chair next to me. But this time, he doesn't hold my hand.

I can see he is as nervous as I am. He clears his throat again.

"Mihika...", he begins.

He is clearly struggling to say something. He seems to be at a loss for words.

"Please, tell me what is going on. I am sorry I don't recognize you. But you need to understand I was..."

"You were in a coma for six months," he completes my sentence, looking at me with an unfathomable expression.

My jaw drops. I was thinking I was out for a couple of days. I never thought of asking anyone how long it really had been. Six months?

"You were in an accident," he says. Then he probably realizes something from the utterly clueless expression on my face.

"Wait. Let me start from the beginning," he says.

III

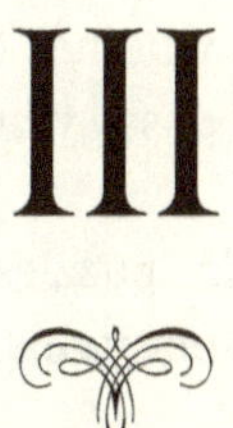

There is a small knock at the door. The door opens and a woman in a crisp white apron enters the room. She nods at the Greek God and then smiles at me. She has a heart-shaped face and a kind expression that can put anyone at ease. Her pointy black hair set in a bob complements her cute features, and somehow, her presence has a calming effect.

"Hello Mihika, I am Dr Arpita, a psychiatric consultant. I want to be sure you are comfortable while Mr Malik tells you everything you need to know," she says, indicating the Greek God with a slight movement of her face in his direction.

Okay, so the Greek God is Mr.Malik. But what does he have to do with me?

I nod at her and attempt to smile. She takes the seat opposite my bed.

The Greek God – okay, Mr. Malik, clears his throat.

"So, Mihika, we know you believe that this year is 2017 and you are in Pune," he says and pauses, to look over at Dr. Arpita. She nods at him, prompting him to go ahead, as I look from one to the other in utter confusion.

"Sometimes, when you are unconscious for a long time, you develop certain neurological problems that are hard to predict. Hard to predict whether they will happen or not, and if they happen, hard to say when they will be cured," he says.

He is still talking in puzzles. I am done with the preamble and I need to know what it is that they think I am suffering from.

"So, you have something that the doctors call 'retrograde amnesia', he says.

I have no idea what that means either. I just keep looking at him blankly, hoping he will reveal what that means.

"You have lost the memory of things leading up to your accident," he says.

I just watch him, not sure what I have forgotten. Well, if I have forgotten, I won't know till he tells me.

"So please don't be shocked, but this year is 2023," he says.

What? 2023?

Have I actually forgotten six damn years of my life??

I look at Dr. Arpita, shock etched on my face. She nods sympathetically.

For a moment, I feel paranoid. Are these people playing some mind game? Is this some conspiracy? But for what? What will anyone gain from lying to me? Or have I forgotten that as well?

"And we are in Mumbai," Mr. Malik goes ahead.

I swallow hard, bracing myself for what more is coming, because his body language tells me there is something else he wants to say.

And then he delivers the biggest shock of my life.

"And we have been married for the past five years", he says.

Suddenly the room seems to be closing in on me. My eyes lose focus and I feel dizzy as if the room has suddenly started spinning around me. I hear cries for a nurse, and I feel two pairs of hands trying to steady me, and helping me lay down before I feel a ringing in my ears, and everything blacks out.

******

I stir in my bed, slowly opening my eyes. I see Mr. Malik seated next to me, looking at me curiously, anxiety written all over his face, as if afraid that I will lapse into unconsciousness at any moment.

For a moment, my mind is blank. I am not thinking about anything. Then suddenly, everything comes back.

2023.

Mumbai.

Married to this Greek God.

My forehead hurts. I put my palm on my forehead.

"Are you alright?" he asks softly.

I sigh and try to sit up straight. He helps me sit propped up on my bed. Then he sits back in his seat and keeps looking at me expectantly.

Sadly for him, I still don't remember him.

"I don't know what to say. I can't remember anything you are telling me. It is unfathomable, how my brain can erase absolutely everything that has happened in the past six years," I say, sounding incredulous even to myself.

Mr. Malik nods his head in understanding.

"I can't imagine what you are going through Mihika. I can't imagine having six long years of my life erased from my memory either. But it is what it is. The good thing is, you are safe, and you are back. There was a point when the doctors had seemed hopeless about your case. They had even counseled me for organ donation, just in case. It felt like you would never wake up. And even if you would, you would be a vegetable. But by God's grace, the worst thing that has happened to you is loss of memory, and I think that is the best we could ask for in the given scenario!" he says.

I nod.

I understand what he is saying. If indeed I had been in a terrifying accident, one that I wasn't expected to come back from, this is like a new lease of life for me.

But what do I do with it when everything around me is unfamiliar? When I have no clue what happened to the life I was living then? How has the world changed so much for me over these past few years?

"Are you sure you remember absolutely nothing during this period?" Mr. Malik asks, doubt flashing across his face as he squints his eyes at me with a slight tilt of his neck.

"Yes, I remember nothing. Zero. Zilch," I stress.

Another expression flashes across his face.

Is it relief? But he quickly diverts the topic, and it's like he never asked me that question.

"So, what do you want to know?" he asks.

And I don't know where to begin! I have thousands of questions for him. And yet, I am not sure what exactly to ask.

How do I figure out my life course of six years with just a few questions??

One month later

I look at my husband from the balcony on the first floor, as he gets into the passenger seat of his indigo BMW and drives away.

I sigh. One more day with nothing to do.

In this one month, I have learned many things about myself. Things that I have seemingly forgotten because of the accident I was involved in. Which I don't remember either.

The doctors say I have retrograde amnesia and my mind has erased the memories of the past six years of my life.

Initially, I was paranoid. It was tough to believe that I had blanked out six long years from my mind.

Because otherwise, I felt absolutely normal. There was no sign of any brain damage that I could sense. And I had memories till the point I could recall. So, it was unbelievable that six years had been totally wiped out from my brain. If at all they had, I would at least have some snippets of memory, right? Our brain isn't a slate that you can wipe words off with a swipe of a cloth after all!

So in the beginning, unbeknownst to my husband and the doctors and nurses (because I suspected if there indeed was a conspiracy going on behind my back, then they were all in it together), I tried to find out if it was 2023 indeed. But it didn't take me long to realize that they were telling the truth. Random strangers, news channels, billboards on roads; everything confirmed the same. So then, well, it must be true! What I find incredulous is, how miraculously my life has changed in these six years! It just seems unbelievable!

My *husband*. This word seems strange. Because according to my memory, I have never been married! So, Mr. Hrehan Malik, is the CEO and co-owner of the Malik group of industries. And my husband of five years.

I am no longer Mihika Roy. I am Mrs. Mihika Malik. That name is going to need some getting used to.

So, one more day with nothing to do. In this huge palace of a house. With servants at every beck and call but no one to talk to!

I sigh. But I don't see any option. My mind flashes back to my past like it does so many times nowadays. The past that I do remember.

I was born and brought up in a lower-middle-class family. Money was always tight in our household, and if I had learned one thing as a child, it was that money is the only gateway to a good life. Something that I would never achieve in this life! Or so I believed! The childhood poverty might have pushed me to pursue a degree in commerce and accounting. I wanted to understand finances better so I could do something about them.

I remember how I used to crave a better life. A bigger house, a big car (can't say bigger because we never had a car to compare with in the first place), designer clothes, branded bags, high-class parties! I used to spend hours sifting through pages of page three magazines, wondering how the lives of these models and celebrity housewives were, and how it felt to be in their shoes.

I was only fifteen when my mom passed away. Then it was just my dad and me. He immersed himself so much in his work, that I hardly ever saw him. But his hard work earned us enough money to pull me through college.

My dad always saw me as a responsibility. A burden he had to bear all his life. He never saw me as a companion. He never shared his grief with me. We hardly ever had a conversation that went beyond what was to be cooked for lunch or dinner.

After college, I should have taken up some accounting job based on my qualifications. But my fascination for the rich class, the other world I could never be a part of, made me apply for a post in an advertising firm. This firm was well-known, and I knew they had endorsed many a celebrity. I don't know what I expected out of the job. But just the thought that I could meet someone rich and famous, someone influential, made me take whatever job they offered. I began enjoying my stint in the advertising firm. I did meet many people I could never have otherwise met. Bollywood actors, actresses, models, fashion designers, famous sportsmen!

All was fine till my dad began behaving weirdly. He started forgetting things. Initially, it was very subtle. But soon he began to do gross things like having lunch twice or going back to his place of work after returning home for the day. Finally, I took him to a neurologist. He was diagnosed with Alzheimer's.

With each passing day, managing him was becoming difficult. He was given voluntary retirement from his place of work. Anyway, he had only a couple of years more to reach retirement age. But his Alzheimer's made it impossible for him to continue doing the job. Using his pension money, I got him admitted to a hospice that cared for the old and debilitated. I felt sad doing this, but I had no option. I couldn't keep him locked up in the house. I couldn't monitor him while I was at work. Here, he was looked after by trained staff and had company his age. This was the best he could get at this age and with his disease.

The facility was located on the outskirts of Pune, yet I managed to meet him at least once a month. That was where I met Nikhil.

A movement at the periphery of my vision catches my eye, bringing me out of my thoughts and back to the present. I turn in that direction.

From here, I can see the path leading to the gate of our enclosed bungalow. Just outside the gate, there are bushes on both sides. A movement amongst those bushes has caught my eye. There is a flurry of black colour and I see someone fleeing.

V

I quickly turn around and rush down the stairs. I dash through the living room on the ground floor and go out and stand on the porch. From here I can see the main gate and the surrounding bushes very clearly. But all is still now. There is no movement.

I am a hundred percent certain there was someone there. They were wearing something black. And they were watching me.

I feel a tingling sensation of fear run along my spine, the hair on the back of my neck standing erect. I retrace my steps and go back into the living room.

Was there indeed someone there? Or is my brain playing games with me?

I feel like I can't be sure anymore.

I had my regular check-up last week, and the ophthalmologist has not yet given me permission to look at screens. So, I can't pass the time surfing the internet or watching a web series, something that Hrehan does most of the time when he is home. So, is there something wrong with my vision?

Deciding not to dwell on it too much, I retreat to our bedroom upstairs. Even if I call it ours, it is mostly mine now. Hrehan sleeps in the guest bedroom on the same floor. He says I should tell him when I am comfortable enough to sleep with him. And I am not sure if that time is ever going to come!

Anyway, I guess only time will tell that. I go to our bedroom, plonk down on the bed, and lean back on the pillows. Since I returned from the hospital, every day has felt like a challenge. Pune has always been home to me. I could never feel lonely there. But Mumbai is new. Or at least that's how I feel. And I am really very curious about the life I have led for these past six years.

Of course, I must credit Hrehan for being the most supportive husband. He understands what I am going through. He understands I have no memory of him. And he gives me my space. Since I have returned from the hospital, he has seen to it that I have been comfortable and feeling at home here. He doesn't do anything that might make me uncomfortable. Which is a lot, I guess, considering he is my lawfully wedded husband.

He has tried to help me get my memories back, in whatever way he could. We sifted through our wedding photographs – a royal wedding solemnized at the Mariotte – a five-star hotel in Juhu. I looked resplendent in a pink and gold sequined lehenga, and I looked so happy!

Hrehan looked handsome in the cream and golden sequined sherwani. Our smiles displayed how enthralled we were. The way we looked at each other, into each other's eyes, tells me how much we were in love. The camera has captured beautiful moments!

And I literally gawk at the number of celebrities that have supposedly attended our wedding! It must have been like a dream come true for me! Alas, I can't remember what it actually felt like!

Then there are pictures from various trips and vacations we have been to these past years – us posing in front of the Eiffel Tower, me sporting a bikini on a beach in Phuket, us clinking glasses on a yacht in Hanoi, Scuba diving in the Maldives, on a night Safari at Singapore...

It seems like somehow all the dreams I had nurtured for so long had manifested. And the tragedy is that I don't remember anything at all!

I keep asking Hrehan questions about my old life that I have forgotten about. He says I was happy being a housewife. I didn't want to work. I don't know why I would have chosen to sit at home and be a housewife. Because the last I remember, I was doing a job. And I was happy doing it!

I asked him about my social circle, and about any friends I may have had. But he says I was an introvert, that I was happy in my own space.

That is hard to believe. I won't call myself an overt extrovert, but I was never an introvert either. I have always had a small circle of friends, be it in college or at work. So, in this rich life stinking of wealth, I had no friend? Not even a single one?

When I decided to snoop around on the texts and messages sent and received from my old cell phone to get an idea about how my life was, Hrehan handed me a brand-new phone, not a smartphone but a simple phone as I am not allowed to see screens yet, with absolutely no contacts saved. My phone was destroyed in the accident, he said. So obviously I had nothing to go ahead with. Since then, I have made just one call to the hospice where my dad is admitted. And the staff has told me he is in good physical health, even though his Alzheimer's has worsened and he doesn't remember anything about his life at all. That's a blessing in disguise, I guess. I will go to see him at some point. But right now, the doctors are skeptical about me traveling anywhere. They feel I might still need medical attention at any time. I need to monitor for the development of any new neurological symptoms, and so it will have to wait.

But more than anything, I want to go to Pune and see Nikhil. I have no idea what happened between us. It is obvious that we broke up at some point. But why or when, I have no idea.

I also had a few friends whom I could meet and find out more about what exactly happened. But without anyone's contact number, it is difficult to go ahead.

I asked Hrehan about Nikhil. But Hrehan has no idea about who Nikhil is. And the surprising thing is, he says I never mentioned anything about a guy called Nikhil.

So basically, I was with Nikhil in 2017. And I married Hrehan in 2018. What happened between these two events? Why did I break up with Nikhil?

My mind goes back to the first time I met Nikhil. Nikhil was a volunteer at the hospice that my dad was in. He would spend two hours every weekend talking to the inhabitants, reading them stories, conducting group activities and games, and sometimes even volunteering in the kitchen. Initially, I thought he was an employee there. I used to visit Dad mostly on weekends and Nikhil would be reading out stories to him. Once when he wasn't around, I asked the nurse on duty about him. She told me he was an engineer who volunteered at the center. Suddenly I felt tremendous respect for him.

The next time we met, after I had visited my dad, we went to the cafeteria together and time just flew by as we discussed everything under the sun.

I felt comfortable talking to him. He told me he worked at Infosys, and his office was not far from mine.

Eventually, we began hanging out on weekdays, after work, and then on weekends as well. Our friendship slowly started taking on a different meaning, and we started dating.

My phone rings, jolting me back to reality.

It's Hrehan.

"Hello", I say. I just saw him off. I don't know what he wants to talk to me about so soon!

"There's good news," he says.

"What?"

"I got a call from the doctor's office. They have sent the result of your latest check-up. So basically, they think you are perfectly fine, well, other than the memory loss. Your eyesight is good. You can now look at screens if you want to. I know you get bored all day with nothing to do. But now you can browse the internet, and watch movies. You can watch movies on the TV screen in our bedroom. And I will get you a smartphone today. I will have it delivered to you before noon," he says.

Wow, I think, finally!

The phone I am currently using is an old Nokia model, which basically saves only contacts and allows me to just call and text.

But now, if I can get a smartphone, I can do something I have been meaning to do for a long time. I can look up Nikhil. I can try to find him on Facebook. I can try to track my old friends from Pune.

"Mihika, are you there?" he asks when I don't reply.

I am just so overwhelmed with emotion!

"Thanks! Thanks, Hrehan," I say.

Just like he promised, a fancy-looking Samsung phone is delivered to me before lunch. It looks like the latest model there is! It also has a SIM card already inserted. I immediately set out to set up the phone. It takes me some time, but when I am finally done following all the setup instructions, I can't find WhatsApp or Facebook anywhere.

The cook is placing bowls of steaming vegetables and rice on the dining table. I look over at her. Her name is Radha. I don't remember her as well, obviously. But the way she always looks at me, well, I can't describe it! It's like she knows something, but can't talk to me about it.

I have tried to have a conversation with her, but hardly ever succeeded. Whenever I ask her about my past life here, it seems like she gives some well-rehearsed answers.

But I can always sense something is off. She avoids eye contact when she talks to me. And she hurries away for some or the other work whenever I try to get information out of her. All my ways of extracting information from her have gone in vain. So I have given up.

"Radha?" I call her now.

She looks at me wearily, probably expecting me to ask some more questions that she has to bat.

"How do you get WhatsApp and Facebook on your phone?" I ask her.

For the first time in the entire time that I have seen her, she smiles a little.

"Madam you need to download those apps. Go to Google Play Store and download," she says.

Oh, right!

"Thanks," I say.

Radha keeps looking at me for a second longer. I almost feel like she is going to say something, reveal something. But then she just turns and hurries off.

I install Facebook.

I have no idea if my previous account is active. Even if it is, I won't be able to reset my password because I don't even remember the password of my email. Although, I do remember my email ID since that was set up long back.

mihikaflower@gmail.com

I decide to take a chance and try logging into my email id. When I ask for instructions to reset my password, it asks for an answer to a security question.

My mind goes blank for a moment.

The question is – What is the name of my boyfriend?

Name of my boyfriend? What kind of question is that? Is that a trick question?

I type Hrehan as the answer.

It's wrong.

Then I type Hrehan Malik.

Wrong!

I think for a few more seconds and then I type Nikhil.

Wrong.

I type Nikhil Gaur.

Still wrong!

What the hell? What is the answer to this damn question!

Finally frustrated, I set about creating a new email id.

mihikamalik1234@gmail.com

Then using this email account, I create a Facebook account.

A simple task like logging into Facebook and seeing the feed and notification tab feels so...good! So normal!

The first thing I do is search for my name. Mihika Roy. And there I am. Looks like I haven't changed my name on my Facebook account.

The profile picture displays me wearing a black cocktail dress, a wine glass in my hand, and smiling widely at the camera. This picture was taken almost a year back, the date tells me.

I start scrolling down.

My Facebook timeline isn't filled with lots of posts or updates about my life.

Most of the posts are images, with philosophical quotes, shared from some other Facebook page.

The majority of the recent posts have similar content.

'Never apologize for being a powerful woman'.

'A strong woman is a woman determined to do something others are determined not be done'.

'A girl should be two things: who and what she wants'.

'God gave women intuition and femininity. Used properly, the combination easily jumbles the brain of any man I've ever met.'

I read the quotes again, confused. Why have I posted such feminist quotes? What were the circumstances that made me post them, I wonder. Was I already out of my happy bubble of having married the richest, the most famous, and the most handsome man ever?

As I scroll further down, there are more quotes.

'You'll learn, as you get older, that rules are made to be broken. Be bold enough to live life on your terms, and never, ever apologize for it'.

'Sometimes it takes a heartbreak to shake us awake & help us see we are worth so much more than we're settling for.'

'Better to put your heart on the line, risk everything, and walk away with nothing than play it safe. Love is a lot of things, but 'safe' isn't one of them.'

I sit back.

Heartbreak? Love is not safe?

What is the meaning of these quotes?

What was going through my mind when I posted them?

Clueless, yet curious, I keep scrolling.

And then I see a photo. It is dated more than a year back. I am partying with four more girls, whom I have tagged. The place is called Club Cobana. We are standing at the bar, drinks in hand, laughing heartily.

I open the image and zoom at each of the faces that are laughing with me in that picture. I recognize no one. But the way we are drinking together, smiling happily indicates that we must have been friends!

So, I did have friends. But then, why is the update dated more than a year back? Didn't we meet after that? And why didn't any of these visit me now?

I check the names tagged. All are strangers to me.

I click on the profile of one Koel Maarva. I don't waste time checking out her profile. I go directly to the messenger.

I quickly type a message.

'Hi Koel. Mihika here. I hope you remember me. Please contact me on 9987628909. It's urgent.'

I quickly press send, before I change my mind.

Then I go back and click on another tag.

Ritu Sharma.

I go to her messenger and send her the same message.

Then I sit back, thinking.

Who are these girls? Why aren't we friends now? And why hasn't Hrehan mentioned them?

"Madam, lunch is ready," Radha calls out.

I am hardly hungry. I tell her to leave, I will eat later.

"You have to take medicines," she says, standing on the doorstep of the kitchen, looking at me uncertainly.

"I will take them," I say.

"Please. They will help you get your memory back," she says, a pleading look in her eyes.

"What is it you think I should remember?" I ask her, feeling slightly irritated.

I don't need a babysitter. I know how and when to take medicines.

"Everything that you have forgotten," she says with a weird look in her eyes, and she vanishes.

I sigh. Talking to Radha is hopeless.

So, I concentrate on the task at hand.

I scroll some more on my feed. There are some pictures from Hrehan's office parties. There are a few pictures taken at different vacations. There is one more picture with the same four girls, again clicked at some party, where we look like we are taking some shots together, dated almost two years back.

And then directly there are pictures from our wedding.

I scroll further down.

I don't remember if I had posted anything while I was with Nikhil. It would be easier to connect with him if he was tagged in one of the older pictures.

I scroll down. But there are no posts with Nikhil.

Just some posts shared from some other pages. And people wishing me on my birthday, year after year. That's it.

So finally, I go to the search option and type Nikhil Gaur.

I see Nikhil's display picture looking back at me.

I feel a surge of emotions, and with trepidation, I open his profile.

And the first post on his timeline reads "Rest in peace, Nikhil".

Shocked, I keep reading the words again and again.

Rest in peace?

REST IN PEACE?

How is that possible? Suddenly I feel as if I am choking. My palms and soles turn cold and I can feel a tingling sensation going down my spine. There is a rush of blood in my ears as I can feel my eardrums and cheeks warming. I swallow hard. Tears prick at my eyes.

How is it possible? What happened to my Nikhil?

I close my eyes and there he is, standing in front of me, smiling his trademark lopsided smile that always made me weak in my knees. He might not be as handsome as Hrehan, but he was the man I loved. He is the man I remember and crave for.

I don't know how much time passes as I reminisce over my old memories, the memories in which I hugged Nikhil, we laughed together, danced together, and snuggled together!

I open my eyes and wipe the tears that I didn't realize had spilled all over my face and are now drenching my neck. I must find out what happened.

So, did I marry Hrehan after Nikhil died? Or did we break up first and then he died?

First, I need to know when he died. And then, how he died.

I sit up straight.

I scroll down the feed, trying hard to ignore the emotions welling up inside me as I read message after message of condolence for Nikhil.

Finally, I read the last message. A post that was posted by one of his contacts, informing everyone of his sad demise. The date is from January 2018.

I check all the comments. People have expressed shock and anger over the loss of a young life. But none of the comments gives me a clue as to what exactly happened.

And surprisingly, there has not been a single post or comment from my profile.

If I knew he had died, which I definitely must have, why didn't I write anything, I wonder.

I scroll below, not knowing what I am looking for. I just want some clue as to what had happened.

And then, just like I have shared posts from other pages, I see Nikhil has shared quotes from other pages too. The only difference is that mine were motivational and feminist quotes, while his are sad and depressing. And of course, mine are more recent while his are just before his demise.

I start reading them, feeling a melancholy spreading in my body.

'She taught me how to love, but not how to stop.'

'It hurts to leave a light on for nobody'.

'Behind every sweet smile, there is a bitter sadness that no one can ever see and feel.'

'The good times of today are the sad thoughts of tomorrow.'

What the hell? What is the meaning of all these quotes?

The last thing I remember must be somewhere around March 2017, when all was well between me and Nikhil.

These posts begin sometime in July 2017 and go up right up to the time of his death, that is January 2018.

So whatever happened between me and Nikhil must have happened between March to July 2017.

I can't think of any sadness other than our breakup that Nikhil is referring to. Looks like he took the break-up too badly.

What about me? Wasn't it amicable? Weren't we still friends? Why did we even break up?

My mind is full of so many questions, that I feel like throwing the phone against the wall in frustration. But of course, that won't help me.

I close my eyes and take some deep breaths. It takes me a few moments to get hold of myself. Then I go back to his 'friends' section. I search for my name. My name doesn't appear on the list.

So, we had unfriended each other on Facebook!

I think hard.

There has to be some way!

I scroll through his friends list, and suddenly I see a name that I recognize.

Ritika Bhaskar.

Ritika was a common friend. She worked in Nikhil's office and we had met at some of his office events where I had accompanied him. She must know what happened. What happened between us and what happened to Nikhil.

I click to open her profile.

Just out of curiosity, I check if I am on her friends list.

Surprisingly, I am not.

I am sure we were friends on Facebook. Then why isn't my old profile on the list of her friends?

Shrugging other thoughts away, I open her messenger.

I quickly type a message.

'Hi, Ritika. Mihika here. This is my new FB profile. I need some help from you. It's a bit urgent. Can you please ping me back? I will explain on the phone.'

Then I sit back. There is nothing more I can do. My eyes feel strained. They are not used to so much screen probably? I keep my phone back on the table and go to have lunch.

*****

That evening, Hrehan returns late. I am fed up with eating alone.

So, I wait for him to have dinner even though it's almost 10 PM.

There has yet been no reply to any of my messages.

"Do you know a girl called Koel?" I ask Hrehan, moving my fork around in my stir-fried vegetables.

Hrehan looks up, his brows furrowed.

"Where did you meet her?" he asks.

"On Facebook," I say, trying to gauge his reaction.

At least he is not denying knowing her. I am waiting to listen to what explanation he tells me.

He just shrugs.

"She was a friend," he says, not looking at me.

"Was?" I ask, my hand holding the fork frozen on the plate.

"Yes. She was a friend. But you haven't seen each other much recently," he says nonchalantly.

"Why?' I ask.

I have now placed the fork on the plate. Food can wait. But I want more information.

Hrehan shrugs again. If he notices that I have stopped eating, he doesn't show.

“I don’t know. You never told me. You just stopped hanging out with them,” he says.

“What about Ritu?” I ask.

Hrehan looks at me wearily.

"Koel, Ritu, Shanaya, and Ayesha. You used to party out once in a while. But since almost a year back, you guys stopped going out together. You never told me what exactly happened," he says.

If he is lying, I will say he is a damn good actor.

“What else did you do today?” he asks, changing the topic.

I sigh.

"I found out that my ex-boyfriend is dead," I say, trying to see if there is any change in his expression that can betray what he really feels.

But he just looks at me confused.

“Who?” he asks.

“Nikhil,” I reply.

Now it’s Hrehan’s turn to place his fork on the plate.

"I have no idea you had a boyfriend! You were single when we met, and we never really discussed your past, other than your parents," he says.

We both resume eating.

We eat in silence for some more time.

“How did we meet, Hrehan?” I ask him.

Hrehan smiles in a patronizing manner.

"What has happened to you today? Why the sudden barrage of questions?" he asks.

"Just tell me," I insist, playing with my fork again.

Hrehan sighs. “We met at the advertising firm you were working at. I wanted a few commercials shot for my company, and your team came to Mumbai to shoot them. I was actively involved as I wanted to have control over the creative aspects. We used to meet daily in the office. And one day, you asked me out for drinks," he smiles.

I smile back, surprised.

"Wait, so you are telling me, I asked you out?" I ask.

"Yes of course," he laughs.

That's weird, I think, but I don't say it out loud.

"So did we go out?" I ask.

"Yes, how could I say no to a pretty girl?" he laughs.

"And then, what happened?"

"Well, everything happened quite fast, if you ask me. We ended up in my bed that same night. And within a month, we were engaged! You wrapped up everything in Pune, left your job, and relocated to Mumbai in the next six months or so. And two months later, we were married. It was a whirlwind romance," Hrehan smiles, a twinkle in his eye.

I just smile back. It is hard to acknowledge when I remember absolutely nothing.

"I never spoke about Nikhil?" I ask then.

Even I can make out how choked my voice sounds.

Hrehan looks at me and sighs.

He extends his hand towards mine and squeezes it.

"Mihika, I know you have been through a lot. Things have changed in all these years, and it is traumatizing to you. I discussed this with your neurologist today and he has suggested you go for counseling..."

"What?" I pull my hand from underneath his. "No, I don't need counseling. I am not crazy," I say, my voice one pitch higher.

Hrehan shakes his head.

"Mihika, counseling is not because you are crazy. It is just to help you deal with the present situation and the stress it is causing you. Plus, the psychotherapy they offer might even help you regain your memories," he says.

That gets me thinking. If the psychologist can restore my memories, then the therapy is worth considering.

“Okay,” I sigh.

"So, I have taken an appointment for you the day after tomorrow, at 11 AM. The psychologist is Dr. Veeksha Bhatnagar. She works at the same hospital you were admitted to. I will message you the contact number and address. You can take the other car. We have a driver, so don’t worry about driving."

I just nod, concentrating on my fork.

"Meanwhile, why don’t you start doing something?" he adds, probably noticing my somber mood, "An empty mind is a devil’s workshop. That is what is happening with you. Your empty mind must be coming up with conspiracy theories to make life more interesting," he laughs. "But our life is plain and simple. Just start living. Get into a routine. Go to the shopping mall. I will install Google Pay on your phone and link it to my bank account. You can buy anything you want to..."

"Wait, what is Google Pay? I don’t need a card to pay?" I ask, confused.

Hrehan laughs.

“No, you pay using your phone. I will show you how,” he says.

I nod. I have a lot to learn.

“Why don’t you join that Yoga class you used to go to?” he asks.

“Which one?” I ask.

“Right. You don’t remember. You went there for two or three months about a year back. You can rejoin that. You might meet some old friends there,” he suggests.

I nod. This sounds better. I need to get out of this house and feel human again.

"Give me the details of the Yoga class," I say, "I will go tomorrow".

Just then, my Facebook messenger pings.

I literally jump and grab my phone to check the messages, forgetting that Hrehan is sitting there, watching me, and well, judging me.

"Whoa! You got your smartphone today and you already have messages you are dying to read?" he laughs, though not in a sarcastic way, more of a humorous kind of way.

I can't risk him knowing who I am chatting to, for some unknown reason, so I just hold my mobile in my hand, tight, fighting the urge to check the message immediately.

"I am just trying to look for the missing pieces of the puzzle that my life has become," I reply, not wanting him to know what exactly I am up to.

"Who just pinged?" he persists.

I pause, thinking how best to answer this question.

"A friend from Pune I knew long back," I say.

Hrehan just nods.

Thankfully he doesn't interrogate me any further, and I try hard not to look as desperate as I feel to check the message immediately.

Finally, after we are done clearing the table and putting away the plates and bowls, Hrehan retires to his study.

I rush to my bedroom, close the door, and with my heart thumping wildly in my rib cage, I open my Facebook messenger.

Ritika has replied.

'How dare you contact me? I want nothing to do with you. DO NOT CONTACT ME EVER AGAIN'.

I read it once, twice, thrice.

What?

Why wouldn't she at least listen to what I want to say?

Is she still angry that I broke up with Nikhil? Wasn't that a long time ago?

She has no idea what I have been through, and that I need her help to get my memory back!

I type another message.

'Ritika please, I need your help. I had been in an accident, I was in a coma for six months and now, after waking up, I have lost my memory. I don't remember anything about what happened between me and Nikhil. Please, I beg you, just talk to me once.'

And I hit send.

The message doesn't get delivered.

Ritika has blocked me!

Frustrated, I throw my cell phone on my bed. I don't know what to do now.

Ritika was my only way to find out about Nikhil. And now I am at a dead end. Neither Koel nor Ritu has replied to my messages.

I sigh. I have nothing to go on.

I should sleep. My brain is exhausted. I will come up with something with a fresh mind tomorrow.

I get up and go to the window overlooking the road below to draw the curtains. There are three streetlights along the stretch of the road that I can see from here.

Underneath the central street light, I see a figure. It looks like a man wearing a cap. He is looking directly at me.

I freeze.

Our eyes meet for a fraction of a second. And then he turns and vanishes in the darkness.

Terrified out of my wits, I rush out of the bedroom, down the staircase, and burst into the study.

"....no, she doesn't know yet and I am not going to...", Hrehan stops his conversation on the phone and looks up at me from his armchair.

Maybe it's the look in my eyes.

Without me saying anything, he tells whoever he is speaking to on the phone that he will call them later.

"What happened?" he asks, keeping his phone aside, getting up and coming near me.

Who was he speaking to? And what was he referring to?

I can't think straight.

"Mihika?" he prompts.

"Someone is spying on me. On us," I say, still out of breath, from the fear or from my running fast down the stairs, it's hard to tell.

Hrehan embraces me in a soft hug.

I take deep breaths, inhaling his musty cologne.

"Relax. Tell me exactly what happened."

We get seated on the sofa opposite the bookcase, and I tell him how I spotted a man in the bushes outside the main gate earlier that day, and how I found a man staring at me from underneath the street light just now.

"The first time it happened, I didn't give it much thought, thinking that I was just being paranoid. But now, I am sure that man was spying on me", I say.

"Did you see his face?" Hrehan asks me.

"No. This afternoon, I hardly saw anything at all. And now his face was in the dark as he was under the streetlight and wearing a cap. But I could feel as we made eye contact because his eyes shone, twinkled, as they were watching me", I say.

"Have you seen him before?" Hrehan asks.

"I wouldn't remember even if I had, right?" I say, stating the obvious.

Hrehan sighs.

"Okay. Don't worry..."

There is a weariness in his voice that is slowly becoming all too familiar.

"Wait, you believe me, right? You don't think this is me going crazy or this is because of some brain damage that I suffered?" I ask, a note of desperation in my tone.

"No, of course, I believe you. I will report this incident to the police station. They will help, probably send a patrolling team every few hours or so. Your case is still unsolved anyways, so it could be linked to that...".

My heart skips a beat.

"Wait, what case?" I ask.

"Your accident case," he says.

"It was a hit-and run, wasn't it?"

Hrehan sighs again, and I see something flash in his eyes. Is it pity? Or is he mocking me?

"It was initially thought to be a hit and run, but later the police believed it was intentional," he says.

"What?" I ask, a cold chill running down my spine.

"You mean to say someone purposefully mowed me down?"

"Yes. That is what the police think," he says.

"But why? Why would anyone want to kill me? And how do the police know it was intentional and not accidental?"

"I have no idea why anyone would want to kill you. And the police aren't a hundred percent sure either, but there has been circumstantial evidence that points at it being a planned crime rather than an accident," he says.

"What circumstantial evidence?" I ask.

Hrehan sighs again. He places his hand on my shoulder.

"Mihika, let's go one step at a time. You have to remember that you are still recovering. And we don't want to do anything that can jeopardize your healthy recovery. I will tell you everything you want to know. But one thing at a time. Today you already have had your share of trauma, knowing about your ex-boyfriend. Now you need rest. You need a good night's sleep. We will talk tomorrow. Okay?"

I sigh. He has a point.

I am on edge today and my body feels like it can't take this any longer. I do need to rest.

"I have sent you the details of the Yoga class. Go tomorrow," he tells me.

"Okay," I say.

Hrehan comes closer and kisses me on the cheek. I smell the cologne again, and suddenly I feel a strong, overwhelming desire for him.

"Sleep well," he says, getting up, unbeknownst to my feelings.

"Good night," I say, and retreat to my bedroom.

*****

The next morning, Hrehan has already left for work when I get up.

I decide not to waste another day sitting at home and getting frustrated. It finally feels good to have a purpose for the day. I take a soothing shower and get dressed in Yoga pants and a tee shirt from my closet.

Radha keeps breakfast on the dining table but I tell her to keep it in the fridge. She stares at me, at the newfound spring in my step but I ignore her as I leave the house.

I get in the car and give the address of the yoga class to the driver. It feels so good to do something so normal, like traveling in a car. I watch as the buildings and trees rush past us. I look at the long road ahead that we are speeding on. I watch the cars around us, all seemingly going to important destinations. I watch people hurrying to work along the footpath. I watch as men and women wait patiently in lines at bus stops. I watch the roadside vendors setting up their small stalls.

The little things. The simple things.

Just as we are rounding a corner, I glance at the back and I notice a red car.

Have I seen that car before? Does it look familiar?

I strain my eyes to see if I can see the driver, but it's hard to tell.

As the driver begins pulling into the parking lot of Corey's Yoga studio, I look back again, hoping the car has left. But I see the red car slowing down behind us, and as we turn, it zooms straight past.

Was the car following us? I should have noted the registration number!

My good mood dampens as a fresh panic grips me.

"Did you see a red car behind us?" I ask Rajan, our driver.

"Which red car ma'am?" he asks, confused.

"Never mind. I will be back in an hour," I tell him.

After getting down, I call Hrehan. His phone goes to voicemail. So I cut the call and text him.

'A red car followed me to Yoga class today,' I type and hit send.

That alleviates my anxiety to some extent, albeit not completely. Hrehan trusts me and he will know what to do.

I shake my thoughts and focus on the task at hand.

I had called the Yoga studio in the morning and booked the class for twice-a-week slots.

I walk up to the building that houses the yoga studio on the second floor.

I try to rattle my brain to see if I can remember this place.

Hrehan said I used to come here sometime back for a couple of months.

But the more I stand there and look at the building, the stranger it feels.

I have absolutely no memory of ever being here!

"Mihika?" I hear a soft voice and startled, I turn around.

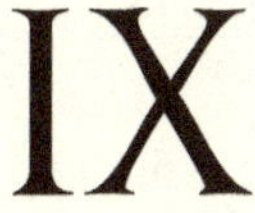

IX

I see a young woman roughly my age, standing there, looking at me expectantly. She is wearing a well-fitting yoga top and track pants that accentuate the curves of her well-toned body. She has tied her long, black, straight hair in a tight high ponytail that makes her already high cheekbones appear even higher. She has a broad forehead and delicate lips.

"Do I know you?" I ask, turning around completely to face her.

The small smile playing on her lips vanishes as her forehead creases slightly.

"You don't remember me?" she asks.

I sigh.

"I was in an accident," I say, not knowing how much this stranger knows about me.

"Yeah, I know...I mean, I read it in the newspaper," she says.

"Right, and I was in a coma for almost six months. And now, after waking up, I can't remember the last six years of my life," I summarise my unfortunate condition in the minimum possible words.

It's hard to spell that out every day.

“What?” she asks, almost gawking at me.

“Yes. So if we have met within the past six years, you have to excuse me, because I have absolutely no memory of the same,” I add.

There is an unfathomable expression on her face. An expression that might as well mean, ‘right, now I get it’. A kind of an understanding expression. But what she has understood, I don’t get. I stare at her, waiting for her to clarify who she is, and introduce herself, but she just keeps staring back, lost in her thoughts.

I clear my throat.

“Oh, sorry. I am Yana,” she says finally.

“Hi,” I reply, feeling awkward, because I don’t know what to say or do next. She probably realizes that and nudges me towards the class.

“Good that you are joining back,” she says as we walk towards the elevator.

“Yeah, I think so. Did I know you from this class back then?” I question.

“Yes, we met here. It was somewhere around a year back, I guess. But you came for just a couple of months,” she says.

We board the elevator. There is a pause as the elevator doors close shut.

“Why did I leave the class back then?” I ask.

Yana shrugs.

"I don’t know. You just stopped coming to the class," she says.

“Oh!” I reply. “Did we stay in touch after I left the class?” I ask.

Yana looks at me for a moment, puzzled.

“I mean, were we friends? Did we chat or call each other?” I clarify.

If that is a yes, maybe she knows a bit more about what my life was like back then.

"Oh, yes, we were friends," she says, "We did chat a bit once in a while. But we both were caught up in our things, you know."

“Oh, right,” I reply, not really sure what she means.

“I mean, we were good friends, we used to meet up regularly when you used to come for the class, but after you left, we sort of lost touch,” she clarifies.

I nod.

Do I sense a pattern? Why is it that I have been friendly with people, and then suddenly cut them out of my life? Were the circumstances different every time?

"And then, one fine day, I read about your accident in the newspaper. That’s it!" she says.

The yoga class goes well, and I feel good that I finally decided to come out of my cocoon and decided to start living my life instead of sitting and mulling and obsessing over things I can’t recall. As we see each other off at the gate of the building, we exchange numbers.

“Can we meet sometime? Over a cup of coffee?” I ask her.

We were good friends at some point in time. Whatever she knows about me from back then, I want to know. And that information cannot be extracted walking to and from a yoga class.

“Sure, ping me anytime,” Yana smiles.

I smile back, and as I walk to my car, I feel the happiness welling inside me.

The endorphins released by Yoga and by meeting an old friend are already healing me!

In the car, I scroll through my uninteresting Facebook feed when my messenger pings.

Excited, I open the notification. It’s from Koel.

'Hi Mihika. Hope you are well.'

That sounds curt, I think. Or maybe I am just overthinking.

'Hi. I am fine. Can we meet?' I type back.

There's a pause, and for a moment, panic grips me as I fear she might block me just like Ritika did.

The small icon says 'typing'. Whatever it is that she's typing, it's taking her forever.

She is probably making up some excuse. I need to tell her about my condition before she turns me down.

So I quickly type *'I have lost memory of the past six years. Can't remember a single thing. Was hoping you could help me get some memories back?'*

I hit send and wait with bated breath.

The typing stops.

There's a long pause. I wait patiently as a honking car makes its way overtaking us.

'Really? Six years? You can't remember anything? At all?' she finally types back.

'Yeah, unfortunately. I don't even recognize my husband! Please help me!' I beg.

There is another pregnant pause.

'How did you find me? Do you remember me?' comes her question.

Now it's my turn to take a prolonged pause. How do you tell someone you don't remember them any longer without sounding rude?

'Sorry, but no. I found your picture tagged on my old Facebook profile. It looked like we all were friends. Us and the two other girls. Whom I don't remember either.'

I don't ask if we all are no longer friends. That is something I want to know about in person. Not over a faceless chat where you can't see the expressions and body language of the person you are talking to, and hence cannot gauge whether they are being truthful or not.

Another pause.

'Ohh...'.

I wait. Is that all she's going to offer? An exaggerated 'oh'?

'Can you help me? I need to meet you' I type back.

I know I sound desperate, but well, I am indeed!

'You mean all four of us?' she asks.

'That would be even better' I say.

'Okay, let me check with the others. I will get back' she types.

I do a small merry jig, even though Rajan is staring at me through the rearview mirror, probably confirming his doubts that I have lost my marbles.

*****

The rest of the day, I make a routine for myself. I eat on time, start watching a series, read a book, and explore Facebook. I even download Instagram but I have no idea how this one works.

Hrehan returns early that evening.

"How was your day?" he asks, plopping his bag on the sofa.

I can feel myself smiling widely as I tell him about my Yoga class and how much I enjoyed it. But I don't mention Yana. I guess, I will have to keep some things to myself until I am sure about everything.

Hrehan has been the ideal husband till now, showering me with all the love, attention, and care he can. And I know I shouldn't doubt him. Rather, I should be thankful to him for everything he does for my sake. But a small lingering feeling at the back of my mind keeps me from trusting him completely. Maybe it's natural to be paranoid or suspect those around you when you have had a neurological injury that left you in a coma for six months and erased your memory of six years! It becomes difficult to believe every word someone says about your life when you can't remember any part of it.

"Let's go out for dinner," Hrehan says, heading towards the guest bedroom to freshen up.

"Sure," I reply without much thought.

Hrehan pauses.

"You don't remember, right?" he asks dryly.

I look at him.

"Remember what?"

He shakes his head.

"Today is our fifth wedding anniversary", he says.

Then, he turns around and heads to the room.

I feel slightly embarrassed. Although, I know it's not my fault, and Hrehan understands. Still, I could sense the disappointment in his tone and his eyes.

X

I shrug away the negative thoughts and decide to focus on the present.

I go to the closet in my bedroom and choose one of the most exquisite dresses that hangs inside. It's a wine-coloured one-piece that goes just off the shoulders with a boat neck and hugs the body till the ankles, breaking into a lacy frill.

I pair it with an emerald necklace. I adorn my reflection in the mirror, wondering what Hrehan sees in me when he looks at me. Does he see the old me? Or does he like this new one better?

We are in our car twenty minutes later, heading towards All Spice, an Italian restaurant that's supposedly my favourite.

Earlier, when we met in the living room after getting ready and walked to the car, there was an awkward silence between us. It felt weird to celebrate the fifth anniversary of our marriage – a marriage that I don't remember at all.

But now Hrehan fills the silence as he drives, telling me what we did on our different anniversaries. Our anniversary tradition, he calls it.

Every anniversary, we used to go to a Chinese outlet for lunch and then to this Italian place for dinner. The Chinese one was his favourite, and the Italian mine, he says.

"Why didn't you tell me this morning? We could have gone for lunch at this Chinese place," I say.

Hrehan laughs. "You hated that place," he laughs some more.

"And I loved this Italian one?" I ask.

"Yes. Let's see if the place brings your memories back," he winks at me.

The Italian joint is a serene place where we sit in a seating arrangement shaped like a cup and saucer. There are only four such seats at four corners of the eating hall.

"This was our favourite seat," Hrehan says.

I can see why it would have been our favourite! It's cozy and secluded, just perfect for a romantic date!

We order Arrabbiata sauce pasta, Vegetable Lasagna and Risotto. We order some red wine.

The ambiance is beautiful, smooth Indie music plays in the background, and as we start drinking and eating, I feel myself unwinding, all the stress I have been piling up inside releasing from my body. The wine loosens up my nerves and the food is absolutely ravishing. I feel myself relax as we chat and laughter flows as easily as the wine.

I excuse myself to go to the restroom as Hrehan calls the waiter, telling me he will settle the bill.

After using the restroom, I steady myself at the sink and close my eyes as my brain is foggy. I shouldn't have drunk so much wine. I have not had alcohol for more than seven months now.

Why didn't Hrehan stop me from drinking so much?

When I open my eyes, I gasp.

In the mirror, I see a man wearing a baseball cap standing behind me, looking into my eyes.

I want to scream but the scream gets stifled in my throat.

I turn around, clutching my hands tight around the edge of the basin lest I should fall because my knees have given way, my legs feel paralyzed with fear and I feel like I will collapse any moment.

The man takes a step toward me.

My teeth are cluttering and I know I must shout for help, but I just can't.

I close my eyes, not knowing what to expect.

Will this man take out a big knife and with one fatal blow, pierce it deep inside my abdomen?

Or will he take a gun out, hold it to my skull, and blow my brains out?

Is he the one who tried to kill me in the hit-and-run, and failed?

Time seems to have stopped, and so has my breath.

I count.

One.

Two.

Three.

When nothing happens for a few more moments, I slowly open my eyes.

The man is standing right in front of me, staring at me. His cap is now in his hand, and his eyes look...worried.

"You don't recognize me?" he whispers.

"Wh-who are you?" I stutter, trying to maintain my composure.

One thing is certain. If he wanted to harm me, he would have easily done that by now.

He doesn't mean to hurt me. He wants to tell me something.

He is still looking at me pointedly. I wait.

He takes a deep breath.

“Don't. Trust. Him,” he says, stressing every syllable through clenched teeth.

“What? Who?” I ask, clueless.

“Your husband. Don't trust him,” he repeats.

“I don't understand...”

"Hey, what are you doing in a lady's washroom?" a woman calls out.

The man looks at her, then back at me.

“Do not trust him,” he repeats.

He thrusts a crumpled note into my hands and dashes out, leaving me utterly bewildered.

It is then that I realize that I am hyperventilating.

“Are you alright?” the woman asks me, worried.

"Yeah, yeah, I am fine," I say, returning to face the mirror.

I stash the note in my pocket.

The woman is still watching me and I don't want to garner any more attention than I already have.

I leave the washroom but my mind won't stop spinning.

Who was the man?

Why did he ask me not to trust Hrehan?

How does he know about me and Hrehan?

Lost in my thoughts, I approach our table, hoping that Hrehan has settled the bill so that we can rush home and I can take a look at what the note in my pocket contains.

But to my surprise, a three-tier cake with a candle shaped like the number five is sitting on our table.

Hrehan is sitting in his seat, his face beaming. As I go near, three hotel staff standing behind Hrehan, whom I had not even noticed, start playing violins.

“Surprise,” Hrehan says, getting up.

He comes around the table and takes me by my hand.

Astounded, and bewildered, I let him take the lead.

He has probably mistaken my expression of shock about what just transpired for my stunned reaction to his surprise.

We stand side by side, cake in front of us, a knife in his hand, the violin-playing staff facing us and playing a beautiful, classical note.

"Happy anniversary," he says looking at me and smiling. He kisses the top of my forehead gently.

Then he takes my hand in his, and together we cut our anniversary cake.

People around clap and cheer, many come and wish us, and we offer cake to everyone around.

Hrehan insists we drink a last glass of wine to toast our future together.

Moments before going to the washroom, I was having the time of my life, or whatever remains of it!

But now, I just can't.

All I keep thinking about is that man and his creepy words, as I plaster a fake smile and go through the motions to appear normal.

I am in a daze when we return home.

I don't know what to believe and what not to believe.

I am completely baffled and confused, and I don't know what to think of Hrehan now.

Although I didn't even know today was our anniversary, he went out of his way to arrange such a nice surprise for me. It was a thoughtful and romantic gesture. Had I not met that mysterious man, I would have been overwhelmed.

But now I am just puzzled. My mind is a mixed bag of emotions. And I don't know what to do!

I feel like slamming my fist into the wall to vent my frustration about not having my own memory and having to rely on people to know what the truth is.

But that will not do anything other than probably fracturing my wrist.

"Do not trust him," that man had said.

If it is indeed true, and if Hrehan is really hiding something, then he is a terribly good actor.

But if it's not, then I am just being an unfortunate loser, doubting my loving and caring husband!

"Thank you for the wonderful evening," I say to Hrehan as we enter the foyer of our house.

I hope my reaction has not dampened his mood, not disappointed him. I tried to look appropriately happy, surprised, and excited.

But I felt none of these emotions.

All I felt was anger and frustration for not knowing anything about my own life!

"You seem... far away," he says, turning to look at me.

“Oh, I am just tired, that’s all. Yoga for the first time...in a long time,” I laugh nervously.

Hrehan nods, thoughtfully.

“You texted me earlier that a red car was following you?” he asks.

“Yes. I think it was following me,” I say.

“Did you note down the numberplate?” he asks.

Now that is an obvious question.

“Unfortunately no,” I reply, feeling defeated.

He sighs.

“It could be related to your accident,” he says. “You need to be careful”.

“Do you think we should report this to the police?” I ask.

Hrehan shrugs. “I am not very sure. But the next time you see that car following you, note down the number plate and we will involve the police,” he says.

“Okay,” I say.

We stand facing each other for an awkward moment.

Then Hrehan comes and takes me in an embrace.

But even this gesture doesn’t relax me.

I can feel how stiff I am. If he has noticed, he doesn’t say anything.

“Good night,” he says.

“Good night”.

The moment I go to my bedroom, I slam the door shut and retrieve the note from my pocket. I open it with trembling fingers.

There are only two lines scribbled.

Ronit

98777889988

I thought there would be some explanation about why I shouldn't trust my own husband.

Instead, there is just a name and contact number.

Who is this Ronit? What does he know about me?

Should I ask Hrehan about him?

Something tells me I shouldn't.

Should I call this man? What if he is lying? What if he is dangerous?

What if he is the one who wanted to kill me in the first place?

Could he be the one who was following me in the red car?

I am now certain he was the one spying on me in the house. But I can't be sure if he was driving that red car.

But if at all he was, why has he been following me around?

And what if he is right?

I have no idea what to do!

One thing is certain. I can't ignore what he told me.

I need to know what this guy knows about us. And why he said what he said.

I take a deep breath and punch those numbers on my mobile dialer.

The mobile number is switched off.

I sigh.

This will have to wait.

I grab my nightwear from the closet and go to the washroom.

I turn on the hot water shower and stand underneath it till I feel my muscles relax under the flowing hot water.

As I lay in bed, sleep won't touch my eyes.

I take my mobile and start mindlessly scrolling on my Facebook.

Koel has still not replied to me. Nor has Ritu.

Just then a thought occurs to me.

Yana said she read about my accident in the newspapers.

That means my accident news must be there on some online news website.

I go to Google and type 'Mihika Malik accident' in the search tab.

The moment I click the button, I get a lot of hits.

Like I thought, all are news articles dated seven months back.

I click the first one.

Wife of multimillionaire Hrehan Malik mowed down by a truck. Condition serious. Accused absconding. Senior correspondent Amit Verma, India News

The wife of multimillionaire Hrehan Malik, Mrs Mihika Malik, 30, was critically injured in a hit-and-run accident. Mrs Mihika has been admitted to Lifecare Hospital, and the doctors have said her condition is very critical, and that the next 24 hours will decide whether she survives or not.

The incident happened in the eerie hours of the morning, at around 2 AM, on the road at the intersection in front of City Mall, when a speeding truck dashed over the victim who was crossing the road with her husband. The truck did not stop to help the victim, and the driver fled with the vehicle. A good Samaritan stopped their car and helped shift the victim to the nearest nursing home where her condition was stabilized, and then she was moved to Life Care hospital for further treatment.

The police are looking for the whereabouts of the driver. They are in the process of obtaining the CCTV footage from the surrounding area.

I look up. The intersection in front of City Mall? What were we doing there at 2 AM, I wonder.

I click another news dated a few days later than the first one.

Mrs Mihika Malik still in a coma.

Senior correspondent Amit Verma, India News

The wife of multimillionaire Hrehan Malik, Mrs Mihika Malik continues to be in a coma after the hit-and-run accident that happened Tuesday in the wee hours of the night in front of City Mall.

The doctors have claimed that she has suffered a head injury and it is difficult to predict when she will come out of the coma. The driver of the truck that hit Mrs Malik is still absconding.

Our informer tells us that the number plate of the truck that the police retrieved from the CCTV footage around the place of the accident was fake, and the driver and the truck, neither have been traced. The question now raised is, why would a vehicle involved in a hit-and-run have a fake number plate? Is there more than meets the eye? Was this accident planned? If yes, why? And was the target Mrs Mailk, or someone else?

Will the police be able to find the perpetrator and do justice to Mrs Malik? That remains to be seen. The police are tight-lipped about this, and so is Mr Hrehan Malik who refused to comment.

I close my eyes. This is more than I can take.

Right from the time I woke up, I believed that I had been involved in some terrible accident. But an accident is an accident after all—unpredictable, unexpected. That is why it is called an accident in the first place!

But after reading these news reports, my mind is clouded with questions and uncertainties.

What were we doing on that road at such an ungodly hour?

Why did the truck driver never get caught? Surely some CCTV footage must have captured him or his vehicle?

And the biggest riddle of all, why was the number plate fake? Why was the number plate fake unless this was planned? And if it was planned, who was the target? Was it really me? Or was it Hrehan?

If I am just the wife of a rich businessman, why would anyone want to hurt me?

Logically, Hrehan had more enemies in his line of work. Could it be someone trying to get rid of him, and they accidentally targeted me?

But how did they know when we would be at that intersection at that odd hour of night?

Unless someone specifically led us there? And why?

Can it be a coincidence? A truck with a fake number plate due to some other reason colliding with me on the road?

What is the probability?

Very meager, if you ask me!

I close my eyes and squeeze them hard. I clutch my temples and massage them.

My brain feels like it will explode and I cannot stop it.

I begin taking deep breaths till my breaths slow down and I can feel my heartbeat, which seemed to have rocketed moments earlier, settling down.

I scroll further. The news articles are more or less similar.

There's just one recent article.

Mrs Malik out of a coma after six months.

Senior correspondent, Amit Verma, India News

Mrs Mihika Malik, the wife of multi-millionaire Mr. Hrehan Malik, who had been in a coma for the past six months after she was mowed down in a hit-and-run accident near the

City mall has regained consciousness.

According to Dr Paresh Rishi, Senior neurologist at Lifecare Hospital, this is nothing short of a medical miracle. Her condition had been so critical, and her head injuries had been so extensive, that there were statistically minimal chances of her survival. Yet, fighting against all odds, Mrs Malik has won her long battle against her brain injuries.

A word of caution though has been issued to her, Dr Paresh said. They are still not sure about the long-lasting effects of her head injury, and she will be kept under observation for her neurological recovery till she is absolutely fine.

The driver who hit her, and his truck, both remain missing, and this is a mystery that as yet remains unsolved. Whether it is due to the mastermind of the person who has done this, or due to police apathy and impotency is yet to be seen.

But the speculation remains as fresh as ever. Was this really an accident? Or an act of revenge?

*****

The next morning, I insist on cooking breakfast, just to make myself busy and distract me from the thoughts that have tormented me all night resulting in an extremely restless sleep.

"Good morning," Hrehan says cheerfully, settling at the dining table.

“You should be resting. Radha is there to cook,” he adds.

“No, I wanted to cook,” I say, as I serve steaming hot paneer paratha onto his plate.

Hrehan inhales the aroma.

“Smells lovely,” he says and delves into it. “So, I hope you remember your appointment today?” he asks, chewing a bite bigger than his mouth can hold.

"What?" I pause, confused.

“Your appointment with the psychologist? I told you the other day?” he says, stopping mid-bite.

I had completely forgotten about it with everything going on!

I am not in the mood to visit a therapist today. I don’t want someone else to dissect the thoughts that I am already dissecting too much myself. I need some distraction.

"She is a renowned psychologist and her appointments are full for months together. We are lucky she squeezed in time for you, of course with a special request from me," Hrehan boasts, unaware of the turmoil in my mind.

“Okay,” I say, reluctantly.

I remember what Hrehan had said when he first told me about seeing the psychologist. He had specified that she could juggle up some memories for me. Which at this moment, seems impossible. So it does seem really worth the try, I guess!

“What time is it?” I ask.

“11,” he replies, busy applying more butter to his paratha.

I observe him as he eats carelessly. I am not sure whether this is the right time to broach this topic or not. But I won’t rest until I have tried to find out more, so I decide to push it.

"How did I get involved in the accident?" I ask, trying to sound as casual as I can, trying to hide the fact that I have spent the entire night researching and then analyzing the same question.

Hrehan stops eating.

“Why do you ask?” he asks me.

I shrug nonchalantly.

“Just curious,” I reply. “You said it was a police case, that the driver was never found. So I was wondering, you know, what were the circumstances,” I say.

Hrehan tears a big piece of the paratha, dips it in the lime pickle, and takes another big bite. It seems like he is chewing the bite forever.

But I wait patiently. Finally, he swallows the morsel and clears his throat.

"You were run over by a truck," he says.

I almost roll my eyes now. Of course, I know that!

"I know, but how? When? Where?" I ask.

Hrehan bides some more time drinking an entire glass of water that he had not touched till now. Why is he suddenly feeling thirsty, I wonder.

"The accident occurred at the town center, near the City Mall," he says.

I wait. I want more. But I can't pester him, so I just keep looking at him, eyebrows raised.

I wait patiently as he gobbles down another big piece of paratha loaded with pickle, and drinks some more water.

"It was nighttime. You probably didn't see the vehicle coming," he says at last.

Night? More like way past midnight, I want to add. But I want his cooperation.

It's anyway too late to tell him that I have already read about it on the internet and I just want to confirm the facts.

Why does it seem like he is hiding something?

"Where were you? Were you with me?" I ask.

"Yes, of course," he shrugs.

"Didn't you notice the vehicle?" I ask.

He stops mid-bite and looks at me with an exasperated expression.

"It happened too fast Mihika. One moment we were talking, crossing the road, and the next moment, you were flat against the pavement, head hit on the footpath edge, blood pooling around, a vehicle speeding away! It just happened in the blink of an eyelid!" he says.

I nod. Somehow this entire scene has flashed in front of my mind's eye, giving me a chill down my spine. We eat silently for some more time.

Finally, I ask my last question.

"What were we doing there? Why were we there?"

"We were celebrating your birthday," he says.

Oh. I never focused on what date it actually was. So it was my birthday?

"Just us? Or was someone else with us?"

Each question is very important to me. I need to know if we went there by ourselves, or if someone did indeed lead us there.

"We were with a few friends," he replies.

Friends? Apparently, I don't have any friends! And whichever friends I had, they broke up with me long ago!

"Which friends?"

"What's with this interrogation early in the morning? What happened?" Hrehan asks, clearly irritated.

"I just want to know, Hrehan. You have no idea what it feels like to be missing out on six long years of your own life," I say.

"That is exactly why I insist you meet Dr. Veeksha, the psychologist," he says, in an irritated tone.

"I will go and see her. But right now, I just want to know the facts. You said I had no friends, and that I was an introvert. That I had broken up with those friends I saw on Facebook. So obviously I am curious about who I was celebrating my birthday with," I say, aware of the agitation in my tone.

Hrehan looks down and sighs.

"I had called a few colleagues from office," he says.

Colleagues from his office?

I was celebrating my birthday with colleagues from his office? Till 2 AM in the morning??

But before I can ask any more questions, he gets up.

He puts his coat on.

"Don't forget your appointment," he says, grabbing his car keys and heading out of the door.

I sit there wondering why he is so hesitant to give me answers to simple questions that matter to me.

Just then, my cell phone pings.

I grab it.

It's a message from Ronit's number.

I open it with trembling fingers.

'Sorry, my mobile was switched off yesterday night. Saw the notification now. Are you ready to meet me? Do you want to know the truth?'

'Yes,' I type quickly.

I can feel my breath becoming heavy and my heart beating fast.

'Meet me at our usual place at 9:30 then' he types.

Usual place? I regularly met up with this guy? We had a 'usual place'?

'I don't know where that is' I type back, unapologetically.

'Oh. So you have actually forgotten everything' comes the reply.

I don't answer. I wait. I don't know why he is so desperate to meet me when I am the one who needs to find out the truth.

'Meet me at Bomie's café at 9:30 sharp' he types.

'Okay'.

Charged with Adrenaline, I quickly jump into the shower. After getting dressed, I am about to call the driver. But then I stop.

I can't take our car and driver with me. Because I don't know whether I want Hrehan to know that I have met with this mysterious guy. Not until I know for sure what he wants to tell me.

I decide to hail an auto from the crossing.

"Not taking the car?" Radha questions, suddenly appearing out of nowhere, as I am about to step out of the house.

"No," I reply, not sure how to dodge her.

"Taking an auto from the crossing?" she asks.

I look at her, dumbfounded.

How the hell did she guess? There is a hint of a smile on her face.

"You used to do that all the time before," she says, the smile still playing on her lips.

"Do what?" I ask.

"Take the auto from the crossing. Not take the car even though it stood there in the garage," she says.

Her face challenges me to read between the lines.

I don't know what to make of this information. I don't know what she is trying to tell me. And I don't have time for this.

"I am in a hurry," I reply, turning around and taking another step out of the main door.

"You want me to call him?" she asks.

I stop in my tracks. What is she talking about?

"Who?" I ask, turning around.

She stares me down for a few more moments.

"No one," she replies and turns around to retreat wherever she came from.

What the heck!

What is the deal with this woman?

She most definitely knows something that she is not letting on.

I will have to grill her one day.

But I don't know how to do that. She somehow intimidates me.

The look in her eyes when she stares me down is fearless.

As if she has some power over me. Like I have something to lose.

What that is, I have no idea.

The other thing is, I don't trust her. Even if I grill her and she tells me something, I don't think I am ever going to be able to believe whatever she says, unless there is some concrete evidence.

I glance at my watch. It's pushing 9. I must hurry. I can deal with Radha later on.

Fifteen minutes later, I alight the auto in front of a cozy-looking café, the Bomie's café.

As I look at the peach and red coloured coffee shop with a giant coffee mug in pink neon lights announcing its name against the door, for the first time since I woke up from the coma, I get the sense of déjà vu as if I have been here. I have seen this place.

I close my eyes, Are my memories coming back?

I stand there, with my eyes closed for just a few more moments. I am hoping to get some vision or something, of the past, related to this café.

But when nothing more happens, I open my eyes and focus on my present.

I cross the road and open the door.

The scintillating aroma of freshly brewed coffee wafts across the room and gives me another wave of nostalgia.

I know this place. I know this smell.

As I scan the almost empty café, I spot Ronit sitting at the last table in a corner.

The moment our eyes meet, he waves at me. We hold eye contact as I approach the table.

Somehow, he doesn't feel scary anymore.

He is smiling at me, a genuine smile that reaches his eyes and crinkles their edges. I smile back, a guarded smile. I still don't know if I can trust him.

I take the seat opposite him. Immediately, probably since the café is almost empty, a waitress approaches us.

"What would you like to order?" she asks.

"The usual," Ronit smiles at her.

"Sure. You guys are here after a long time," she says, smiling at us and retreats.

So she knows 'us'.

"What is the usual?" I ask Ronit.

"Two Café Latte, one with more sugar and one with more cream," he smiles at me.

He is right. I do like Café Latte with more cream. And the fact that the waitress here knows means that we have been here, and ordered the same for at least more than a few times.

"How are you, Mihika?" Ronit asks me, jerking me out of my thoughts.

He tries to place his hand over mine, but I retract it. He takes his hand back.

"I am fine," I reply.

I wait. Ronit clears his throat.

"You don't remember absolutely anything?" he asks then.

"Nothing from the past six years," I reply.

Ronit's eyebrows shoot up, creating a tangle of furrows on his forehead.

"Six years?" he gasps.

"Yes," I reply. "I don't remember getting married to my husband even," I add.

Ronit laughs dryly.

"That's probably a good thing," he says.

Enough with the beating around the bush. I am losing my patience.

"Why did you tell me that day not to trust my husband? And why have you been spying on me?" I ask him, point blank.

The waitress arrives with our coffees, just the way we like them.

We wait patiently while she carefully places the correct mugs before us.

I am observing Ronit. He looks...hurt?

"You do realize that whatever has happened cannot be told in a summary in five minutes, right?" he says once the waitress is safely out of earshot.

"What do you mean?" I ask.

"I mean, when things happen, they happen in a logical sequence. Things happen due to changing circumstances.

We behave as our surroundings change. Suddenly one day if you decide to ask only the result, without understanding the process that led to it, without trying to know the circumstances around it, then the end result will seem impossible, or unacceptable," he says.

I don't understand a word of what he is saying. I keep looking at him blankly, waiting for him to speak in a language I understand.

"To tell you in short, I can't tell you why I said what I said without giving you the background, without telling you everything that happened that led me to say it. Because otherwise, you will never believe me," he says.

Ok, now things are making a bit of sense.

"So, tell me everything in detail. Tell me right from the beginning. Tell me when we met first, and what you know about me and my husband. Tell me about my past life that I have forgotten about," I plead. Beg almost.

Ronit takes a sip of his coffee.

"Drink yours before it gets cold. You don't like your coffee cold," he says.

He is right. I need my coffee steaming hot.

I take a sip too, and wait.

Because right now, coffee and its temperature are the least of my worries.

"I am a private detective," he says, after taking a few sips of coffee.

"Okay," I reply, eager to know more.

"You hired me about a year back to investigate your husband," he says.

What?

"Investigate my husband? Why?" I ask.

"You believed that he was having an affair with someone," Ronit says.

I pause to digest that.

I suspected Hrehan of having an affair?

"So, was he?"

"Most likely," Ronit says.

"Most likely? What does that mean?"

"I mean, we didn't have any concrete proof, but you can say we did manage to get circumstantial evidence," he says.

I am struggling to believe this. The husband, who has been so loving and constantly caring for me, was having an affair?

Should I just leave this place right now?

Why should I believe what this man is telling me? What is the proof that he is not lying to take advantage of my amnesia?

But I decide to listen.

Whether or not to believe whatever he says, I will decide.

"So who was he having an affair with?" I ask.

"Someone from his office," he replies.

"Who?" I ask.

"You won't remember her, right?" Ronit points out.

"I want the name of the woman," I say.

"Anaisha. She is your husband's secretary," he replies.

This is like a blow to my gut.

Even if I don't remember getting married to Hrehan, I have accepted him as my husband. It has been difficult to do that, and it's not like it has happened overnight. It has been a process. A slow process. And every day, I accept him as my husband a little more.

Now, this new information feels like a big crack in the carefully constructed emotion that I have nurtured over the past month.

And if Ronit is giving me a name to back his story, the chances that he is lying seem less!

"Is she still working for him?" I ask, trying not to show what emotional turbulence my mind is going through.

"I am not sure, but most probably yes," Ronit says.

"Didn't I confront him? Didn't I do anything about it?" I ask.

Ronit clears his throat, as if there is something even more difficult than what he has already told me, yet to be revealed.

"Things...changed," he says.

I don't understand.

"What things?"

"Things...between us," he replies, now looking at me pointedly.

"What do you mean?"

He sighs.

"This is just so difficult," he says, hanging his head down.

I wait. Whatever it is, however difficult it may be, I need to know. I want to know.

"We got closer," he says then.

I am shocked.

Does he really mean what I think he does?

"What do you mean we got closer?" I persist.

"We got intimate. We had an affair. You realized you wanted to be with me, and decided to leave him. Exposing his affair seemed pointless. We made plans to help you escape from him," he says.

What?

Is this some kind of a joke, I wonder.

Something about this entire thing feels off.

I hired a private detective to spy on my husband because he was supposedly having an affair. And then I ended up having an affair with him?

It seems ridiculous even in theory.

"It wasn't just the affair," he then says, probably getting a hint of what is going on in my head.

"What do you mean?"

"Your husband was abusive. He used to gaslight you. He used to emotionally manipulate you. and sometimes even..."

"Sometimes what?"

"He hit you on a few occasions," Ronit says finally.

What? This is absolutely unbelievable.

The soft and gentle-mannered husband I see at home used to gaslight me? Physically and emotionally abuse me?

"You used to cry for hours and I used to console you. One fine day, you were determined to get out of the marriage. We decided to get you away from your husband," he sighs.

It is difficult for me to fathom this. I listen to him, my mind numb.

"For that, you would first need to leave your job..."

"Wait. What job?" I ask, perplexed.

Hrehan has told me I preferred to stay at home, and not work. Then what job is he talking about?

"You used to work in the accounting department of your husband's company. Didn't he tell you that?"

I had no idea.

"No," I say.

"See? I told you not to trust him," Ronit says. "The thing is, Hrehan is a manipulator. He never let you have any close friends. He always did something or the other to alienate you from your friends. He alienated you from your relatives. He wanted full control over you, over your existence. When we first met, you told me that you had wanted to do a job in one of the leading accounting management firms in Mumbai. But Hrehan had made you join his business, so that he could keep tabs on you, and you would still depend on him for your financial needs," Ronit says.

I can't fathom whatever Ronit is telling me. But at the same time, I think there is an inkling of truth to everything he says.

Hrehan is very reluctant to talk about the accident, and I had to probe so much to just get that information out of him! He never mentioned the friends I had, and had I not created a different account on Facebook and gone through my own profile, I would probably never have known about those friends I used to hang out with. When I asked Hrehan about them, he told me that I had broken up with my friends, and he said he didn't know why. That seems impossible, doesn't it? If I was so close to the four girls, and if something drastic happened that would make me break my friendship with all of them, wouldn't Hrehan know? Wouldn't he care to know? Or he didn't simply because he was the reason? Was he the one who made me alienate my own friends?

Since I returned from the hospital, he hasn't taken me anywhere to socialize. Is that his way of keeping me isolated from the rest of the world and holding me under his control?

Coming to think of it, he never even offered to take me to see my dad! I know the doctors have not permitted me to travel, but he has not shown any concern either! He didn't give me a smartphone till a few days back on the pretext that my doctor had said no to any screen, and I have trusted him. What if it was his way of keeping me away from social media for as long as possible?

And the most important thing is that he never told me I worked in his company! Why would he hide that from me? It just makes no sense!

I don't understand now, whether Hrehan is the hero of my life or villain?

Whenever I ask him about Nikhil, he says he doesn't know who Nikhil was, and that I never mentioned him. But that again, seems absolutely impossible. Nikhil was a big part of my past. Even if we broke up for whatever reason, I would definitely have told Hrehan all about it at the beginning of our relationship, wouldn't I?

And then a terrifying thought occurs to me. What if Hrehan was behind our break up? And what if Hrehan was responsible for whatever happened to Nikhil?

XIII

Almost an hour later, my mind is clouded with thoughts as I enter the hospital for my psychologist's appointment.

After meeting with Ronit, I had to rush home in an auto and take the car to the hospital. If Hrehan is indeed a control freak about me, he will keep tabs on my activities.

Is that why Radha said that I used to take the auto from the crossing all the time instead of the car? Did I do that often to dodge Hrehan because he kept keeping tabs on me?

But then she asked me if she should call '*him*'. Who did she mean?

I have to wait for about ten minutes before I am ushered into Dr. Veeksha Bhatnagar's office.

I have already formed an image of the psychologist in my mind's eye, and really, she is just like that - a perfect stereotype!

An old lady with fiery white, silvery hair that creates a crown around her long elongated oval-shaped face, a pair of golden rimmed specs from above which she is peering at me with squinted eyes, a crisp stark white starched saree with borders embroidered in light pink and green colours, a big black bindi adorning her large forehead, and huge, multicolored beads adorning her ears, neck, and wrists.

She is seated behind a Mahogany desk, and the wall behind her is a testimony to all the various certificates of training and excellence credited to her.

“Good morning Mrs. Malik,” she greets me as I enter.

“Good morning, please call me Mihika,” I smile, as I enter the room slowly.

I look around the room. Her office is painted in vivid, vibrant colours – Magenta, purple, bright yellow, fiery red, orange - with a wall adorned with giant-sized pictures of landscapes shot at various exotic holiday destinations – Italy, Peru, Croatia, Santorini!

I look around for the typical psychologist’s couch on which I am supposed to sleep while she conducts my session but there is nothing of that sort.

There’s just a coffee table surrounded by comfortable-looking cushioned chairs.

Dr.Veeksha gets up from behind her desk and ushers me to sit on one of the cushioned chairs. She takes the seat opposite me. She has a pen and writing pad in her hand. As she catches me eyeing the same, she smiles.

“I am a bit old school,” she says.

Her voice is slightly groggy, but it suits her personality. I sit back and wait for her to begin.

Dr. Veeksha clears her throat.

"So Mihika, I have gone through your files and I have learnt that you suffer from retrograde amnesia," she says, peering at me from above her golden-rimmed glasses.

“Yes,” I sigh. “No memory of the past six years of my life,” I reply.

She nods thoughtfully.

“I get how difficult it must be for you to cope with this,” she says.

Especially when you have no clue whom to trust, I want to say. But I just nod.

"So what do you want me to help you with?" she asks.

I pause for a moment. Venting out everything that is threatening to explode inside me seems the best way to be free. But that won't be of any help until I figure out what exactly is happening to me. And the only way that can happen is if I can remember what has happened in these past years that have been wiped out from my memory.

Secondly, right now, I feel paranoid. I don't know whom to trust. And so, I cannot tell everything that is happening around me to anyone. Not even my psychologist, however kind and sincere she may seem.

"Is there any technique that can bring my memories back?" I ask her.

Dr. Veeksha looks out of the window on the right-hand wall, that overlooks the busy road beneath, and she seems deep in thought.

"Usually, patients with retrograde amnesia do not get their entire memory back. I am not saying this to disappoint or dishearten you. I just want to put the facts in front of you," she says, now looking at me.

I nod.

"But they do, eventually get bits and pieces of their memory back. How soon or how later that will happen, no one can predict," she says.

"Okay".

"So tell me, have you recalled any memory from these past six years that you have forgotten about?" she asks.

I close my eyes and think hard. The last thing I remember is being with Nikhil. I have absolutely no memory of this life here, in Mumbai, with Hrehan.

"No," I say.

Dr. Veeksha sighs.

“Sometimes certain memories get triggered by visuals or audio. Or even aroma sometimes...”

"Yes, I do remember something...very vaguely. I went to a coffee shop today. And even though I didn’t get any specific memory back or flashback of any kind, I just felt like I had been there before, sort of a deja' vu, you know? The place, the aroma, all seemed familiar," I say, suddenly remembering how I had felt this morning.

"Great. That’s a good start. So now we know that at least some of your memories can be recovered by triggering them with familiar locations, sounds, and smells. Because your subconscious mind still remembers what your conscious mind has forgotten. Sometimes, a simple touch may elicit a memory..."

Touch! Yes, I remember feeling a sense of familiarity when Hrehan touched me while I was in the hospital.

“...our body responds to certain people’s touch in a specific way. So for people whom you have forgotten, but who are close to you, a simple handshake, a hug can elicit a certain memory that would otherwise not be elicited,” she says.

From the time we came back from the hospital, Hrehan has hardly touched me. Yet, I remember the strong desire I felt for him the other night. Where did that come from? Will touching him elicit any more memories for me?

“So I want you to try to visit those places you used to visit before you met with the accident. Visit that coffee shop again and try to see if you can recall something – anything – related to the place, and probably the people you met there. Meet the friends you had made over these past six years, not just to get information from them, but to see how your subconscious reacts to that experience.”

I nod. What she says is making complete sense.

"Our brain is magical, Mihika, and you just don't know what miracle it can create. So give it maximum opportunities for the same," she says.

We sit in silence for some time. I let her words wash over me as I take them in.

She is right. If I want my memory back, I have to make an effort.

But I have a few questions for her.

"Isn't there any psychotherapy technique that can help?" I ask.

Dr. Veeksha looks thoughtful for a moment.

"See, there is no foolproof way wherein we can guarantee you getting back your memories. Yes, there are different ways of doing so, and we can try them. But you may or may not remember things."

"I understand. But we can try them, right?" I ask, feeling hopeful.

"We can try some therapies to recover your memories. There's cognitive behavioural therapy. There's neurobiofeedback. But I think hypnotherapy will suit you the best," she says.

"I am willing to do it," I say.

I am ready to do absolutely anything to try and get my memory back.

"It's not that simple Mihika. You must understand that in hypnosis or age regression therapy, as we call it, you may uncover certain traumatic memories that your brain has suppressed consciously as a coping mechanism. Hypnotherapy sessions can be greatly challenging and grueling to go through, especially because when you go into the regression, you don't just remember the event, you live it once more. And if it is a traumatic event, you will feel the pain as if it has occurred fresh. This can be a truly and extremely, emotionally numbing and draining experience," she says.

I take a pause. Is it really possible that my brain has blocked out these six years because of some severely traumatic event? Does it have anything to do with Nikhil?

But my marriage to Hrehan seems otherwise! In the pictures of our marriage, which must have been just a few months after Nikhil's demise, I look happy and normal! Whatever it is, however traumatic it may have been, I need to know it. Because not knowing anything is proving too traumatic for me right now.

"I understand," I say.

"Okay. Then I will give you the next appointment for our first hypnotherapy session. You have to understand that you will need many such sessions, and there is the possibility that you might not remember anything in the first few sessions."

"I understand," I say.

The prospect of getting even a small part of my memory back is making me ecstatic.

"We conduct these sessions in our hypnotherapy suite. You will have to sign the consent form. Is Friday fine? Same time?" she asks.

The earlier the better.

"Yes," I reply.

"Okay," she says, jotting down furiously in her notepad.

"Till then, try to do the homework I told you. Try to visit familiar places, and meet familiar people – familiar as in those you were familiar with before but have forgotten about now. And see if any new memory is stimulated. If you succeed, we can take that elicited memory as the base for our hypnotherapy session. That way, we increase the chances of making it successful," she says.

As I leave the hospital, I feel happy I agreed to Hrehan's suggestion of visiting the psychologist. I can't wait for the hypnotherapy session.

And till then, I will do exactly what she asked me to. I will visit my Yoga class and meet Yana once more. I will meet Ronit again at the same coffee shop. And most importantly, I will visit my workplace – Hrehan's office.

Before visiting Dr Veeksha, I had thought I would confront Hrehan tonight about lying to me. But now I realize that wouldn't be a wise thing to do.

If he is really hiding something, he can't know that I am onto him. The more unalert he is, the more likely he is to slip up. Even if I do confront him, I must do that tactfully, without raising suspicion. I have to figure out a way of doing that.

With a firm resolve, I walk towards my car.

Just as I sit in the car, my cell phone pings.

It's a message from Koel.

'Are you free to meet today night for dinner?'

Great!

'Yes. Are we five meeting?' I type back, excitement coursing through me.

'We all except Ritu' she types back.

Okay. I don't know why that is, but this is good.

'Can we meet where we used to meet before?' I ask.

I have to visit old, familiar places.

'Do you remember it?' she asks.

Obviously not, but I can check it from the check-ins from Facebook!

'No. I just want to see the place as I don't remember anything right now' I reply.

'Okay then. Meet u @Shamiyana at 8 PM sharp'.

'Done'.

On my way home, I sense something.

It's like a sensation at the back of my neck that I can't ignore. I turn around in my seat and notice the same red car following me again.

What the hell!

It definitely can't be Ronit. Why would he stalk me for no reason when I have already met him, listened to whatever he wanted to say, and promised to meet him once more since I had to rush for the psychologist's appointment?

So then, who is it? And why are they following me?

I try to see who is in the driver's seat but it is difficult to deduce.

But then I quickly see the number plate, and I store it in notes on my cell phone.

MH 01 2536

I don't know what I will do with this number plate.

Should I go to the police? Should I give it to Hrehan?

Hrehan had asked me if I had noted the number plate when the car had followed me to the Yoga class. But now, after everything Ronit has told me, I don't know whether I can trust him or not.

Ronit is a private detective, he had said. Should I give it to him instead? Can I trust him?

I keep sneaking glances at the car following us, till it disappears one crossing before the one that leads to my house.

That evening, Hrehan returns home by 6 PM. I haven't texted him or called him.

I just want to speak to him face to face, so that I can see his body language and facial expressions while doing so.

"How was your session today?" he asks, flopping down next to me on the sofa.

I am watching him, and somehow, when I look at him, when I look into his eyes, I can't believe a word of what Ronit has said!

Hrehan doesn't look like the man who would try to control, manipulate, gaslight, or alienate me from others! He looks so normal! And there is indeed a kind of warmth in his eyes that one has for his or her loved ones.

Yet, I have to tread carefully. If at all whatever Ronit told me is true, I have to figure it out without Hrehan suspecting.

"It was good. Thanks for recommending her. I know I was reluctant to go but the visit definitely helped," I reply, smiling.

"That's great!" Hrehan replies, absent-mindedly tugging at his tie to loosen it.

"Umm, actually, you know what? We did a small exercise today," I say.

"What was it?" Hrehan asks, still fidgeting with his tie with one hand and checking something on his cell phone with the other hand.

I wait. I want his undivided attention when I speak.

Finally, when he realizes I will not go ahead until he pays me his full attention, Hrehan looks up, placing his cell phone on the sofa.

"It was an exercise to see if we could juggle up any of my memories," I say, stressing every word and observing him carefully to see how he reacts. I know I am treading on fire, but it is worth the risk.

Hrehan sits up straight and a dark shadow passes over his face.

"And? Did you?" he asks, now his full attention on me.

He has even given up loosening his tie, which now hangs limply like a noose around his neck.

"I didn't exactly have any memory back. But I did have a dream-like state where I saw something. I don't know if it's a memory or if it was indeed a dream..."

"Are you talking about hypnotherapy? Did Dr Veeksha do hypnosis on you? On your first visit?" Hrehan questions, his brows furrowed.

Ohh! I didn't think of this. Hrehan would definitely know that no psychologist would directly do hypnosis at my very first session.

"She did suggest hypnotherapy, and I have an appointment for the same on Friday. But today, it was just a mind exercise of sorts, where she made me try to remember things based on my subconscious memory".

My fingers are crossed and I just hope Hrehan believes me and doesn't go to cross-check with Dr Veeksha.

And I hope she takes the confidentiality clause seriously.

I could have done this confrontation after our actual hypnotherapy session. But I can't wait till then to ask Hrehan why he lied about me never working when I had been actually employed in his very own office.

"Okay. So what did you remember?" he asks, not questioning me any further about hypnosis.

"It was very vague. I saw myself seated in a sort of a cabin, at a computer, tapping at the keys, and when I looked up, I saw you in the doorway. You were in your office attire. And it felt like I was working there, you know?" I pause, giving him time to digest this information.

Hrehan's eyes soften as he nods slowly.

"So, was this a memory, or...." I leave my question hanging in the air.

"Yes, it was a memory. You were working at our company," he says.

So, he did lie to me!

But I don't act shocked. I act surprised.

"Really? You never told me! In fact, you categorically told me that I was happy being a housewife!" I say, looking at him, trying my best to sound like I am just curious and not making an accusation.

"I told you this because I didn't want you to join back till you were completely, neurologically recovered. You worked in our accounts department, and that job is stressful. I didn't know if after waking up from a six-month-long coma and having amnesia for the preceding six years, whether it was advisable for you to work in a stressful environment. I even discussed this with your neurologist, and he told me to take it slow."

Ok, that makes sense, but then, why lie? He could have told me the truth! That I was working, but right now, I wasn't fit to join back as yet!

"I know what you are thinking," he says further. "You are wondering why I lied to you. The reason is, Mihika, that you are very stubborn by nature. If I had told you that you had a job but shouldn't go yet, you would never have listened to me. That's why I lied to you. It's not like I was taking advantage of your amnesia. I was doing that to protect you. It was a white lie. A lie told with good intention. A lie meant to result in something good," he says.

I nod in understanding. Everything he says makes sense.

XIV

Now I wonder how true it is that we should never believe a story unless we have heard both sides of it.

The fact remained the same. I had been working for Hrehan's company and he lied to me about it. Ronit portrayed this fact as if my husband was a liar and a manipulator who wanted to control me. And Hrehan explained it to be an act out of love for me. To protect me.

And after listening to both versions, I feel like I trust Hrehan more!

But of course, I can't make an opinion based on one incident. I have to tread carefully.

"Dr. Veeksha believes that one way of getting my memories back is to visit the places I have been visiting these past few years, meet the people I know from these past years, to see if any sight or smell," or touch, I almost add, but I bite my tongue and proceed, "triggers a forgotten memory. So I was thinking of going to the office along with you, just to see if the presence of familiar surroundings can trigger any memory?" I ask.

Hrehan sighs.

"It's too early for you to be joining back. It's hardly been a month since you woke up. You are on so many neuroprotective medicines, including anti-seizure medications. This is not the ideal time for you to join back," he replies.

"I am not talking about joining back. I will just accompany you. I will visit my old workplace, my cabin, meet my colleagues, and just hang around. If that can trigger any kind of memory, it will be worth a shot, won't it?" I ask.

Hrehan hangs his head in defeat. But then smiles.

"See what I meant when I said you are stubborn? Now you know why I lied to you?" he says, smiling.

I smile back.

"Okay, we will go together tomorrow," he says, as the tie finally comes off his neck.

I do a small mental merry jig. This is one small victory for me.

"So, what do you want to have for dinner? Shall we order something?" Hrehan asks getting up from the sofa to go and freshen up.

"Oh, sorry I forgot to tell you. I am meeting my friends for dinner tonight," I say.

Hrehan stops in his tracks.

"Which friends?" he asks, his brows knitted tight.

"The ones I found on Facebook. Koel, Ayesha and Shanaya. Ritu is not joining," I say, feeling it very weird to call them friends when I don't even know what they look like.

"Are they ready to meet you?" he asks, doubt written all over his face.

"Yes. I told Koel that I have lost the memory of these past six years. So she agreed to meet."

Hrehan nods with a serious expression.

"Hrehan, do you have any idea why we all split a year back?" I ask.

Hrehan looks at me. The look on his face tells me he knows. He knows something.

"No," he replies stoically.

One more lie.

Is it again a white lie? What is he protecting me from?

"But whatever it was that broke you all up, must still exist, right? Are you sure you want to meet them?" He asks.

"Yes. It is a part of the mind exercise Dr. Veeksha has told me about. It might help me to meet familiar people, at a place we often went to, to try to elicit something in my brain," I reply.

"Where are you meeting?" he asks.

"Shamiyana, one of the places we usually hung out at," I say.

Hrehan narrows his eyes at me, and I don't know what exactly he is thinking.

"You sure you don't remember absolutely anything?" he asks.

I am stumped.

"Why would you ask me that?" I ask.

Is he doubting my amnesia? Why would I pretend to be amnestic...unless....unless I had something to hide? Did I have something to hide? Something he knows about?

Hrehan shrugs.

"Sorry, it's nothing," he says. "Why isn't Ritu joining? She was your best friend amongst those four".

I shrug. "I have no idea. Let's see what I find out tonight," I say.

"Anyway, take the car and driver with you. Have a good time," Hrehan says, as he starts retreating to his bedroom to freshen up.

"There is something else," I say.

I have decided to trust Hrehan. After this encounter, I am still not convinced that Ronit is telling me the truth. So right now, I will give Hrehan the benefit of the doubt and trust him.

"Yes?" Hrehan pauses and turns again.

"That red car was following me today too. I couldn't see who was driving, but I have noted down the number," I tell him, opening the Notes app on my cell phone where I have saved that number.

"Was it the same car?" he asks. Worry lines crease his forehead again.

"Yes. I recognize the make of that car," I say.

"Ok," he says thoughtfully, taking a photo of the number saved on my notes. "I will forward this to Inspector Ashwin, the investigating officer in charge of your accident case. Let's see if he can help".

At sharp 8 O'clock, I reach the venue Koel told me to reach.

Shamiyana.

I pause outside the building and take a look. It's a three-storey building decorated entirely with Neon lights that light up alternately, making my eyes hurt.

A big sign up in the air reads *Shamiyana* in bloody red colour, and there's a cut out of a full glass of wine next to it.

I close my eyes. Does this place juggle any memory?

I try to focus my mind on the task of trying to bring back any memory I can have about this place.

And then it happens.

For a moment, I get a sense of Déjà vu, and suddenly it's like I am in a parallel universe.

I am here, in this very place, but I am walking along the road, laughing hard, with four girls laughing next to me. I can feel myself feeling tipsy, yet very ecstatic. Their laughter echoes around me. One of them slides her hand into mine, and I hold her hand back, tight.

And that's it. I open my eyes.

My body is flooding with adrenaline.

This is the first flashback I have had since waking up.

I had felt something familiar in the coffee shop this morning too, but I didn't remember anything. It was just a feeling, no real memory.

But focusing my mind to bring up memory by triggering it with something familiar, an exercise Dr. Veeksha told me could help, is actually working!

I even felt what it felt like that evening as I walked, drunk, with my four friends!

That feeling of ecstasy still lingers, as I make my way inside.

This place looks like a very happening place, teeming with the teenage crowd. It's full even though it's a weekday. It smells strongly of fried food and smoke. The music is loud and the DJ is playing some unknown English numbers.

And this smell carries a wave of nostalgia over me.

I close my eyes again, clutching the barricade next to me.

But this time, it's just nostalgia, a feeling that I have been here before.

No concrete memory.

I open my eyes and walk further ahead.

Before coming, I checked Koel's display picture twice, trying to memorize her face. Because otherwise, how will I find them?

It doesn't take me long to spot the two girls sitting at a table in the far corner.

Koel waves at me. I wave back, and I am suddenly feeling conscious.

It is a very odd feeling.

These girls know me. But I do not know them at all. What will I speak to them about? Will I get along?

My heart beats in trepidation as I approach the table.

"Koel?" I say to the girl who looks like the DP I memorized.

"Yes," she smiles and motions me towards one of the chairs.

I get seated and smile at both of them.

"Shanaya," the other one says. I smile at her too.

We all exchange polite smiles. Too polite.

Koel looks absolutely gorgeous, with waist length, jet black, wavy hair, and full lips. She is wearing a tight-fitting black dress that threatens to give way at any point, but she doesn't seem worried about that happening. She looks comfortable in her own skin.

Shanaya looks simpler, with her curly brown hair tied up in a high bun. She's wearing a flowery sundress and looks strangely out of place.

"You don't remember anything then?" Shanaya asks me.

Both of them are eyeing me skeptically.

"No. Like I told Koel, I have forgotten everything that happened in the last six years of my life," I say.

"It must seem weird, right? Because you look so normal," Koel says.

Sometimes it is easier to have a physical disability. Because people don't think that you are pretending or faking.

They believe when they see it.

How do I make people see my amnestic brain?

I shrug.

"The last memory I have is of me six years back. I don't remember Hrehan. I don't remember our marriage," I tell them.

They exchange a look.

From the way they are looking at me, eyeing me, and their tone, I have already started regretting coming here.

I came in the hope of meeting long-lost friends, trying to reconnect with them, finding out what went wrong between us, and trying to correct that.

But they don't seem to have come with any such intention. It almost feels like...like they are mocking me. And they just came here to judge me and laugh at me!

A waitress interrupts the awkward silence that has started threatening to take over our table.

Koel and Shanaya order Vodka shots and some starters. I settle with Virgin Mojito.

"So..." Koel begins, trying to clear the awkwardness by clearing her throat, though her face is set in grim, arrogant lines.

"What exactly do you remember then?" she asks.

Shanaya looks at me curiously.

"Like I told you. It's an absolute blank. I don't remember anything at all," I say.

I am getting slightly annoyed now. But I decide to try and maintain my composure. I need their help. So I have to be patient.

"What's your last memory?" Shanaya questions.

I shrug. "There is no absolute last memory. But in my head, I am somewhere at the beginning of 2017," I reply.

They both gawk at me.

The waitress places our drinks and starters on our table.

We sit in silence for some time, nibbling the starters and sipping our respective drinks.

"So," Koel interrupts the silence between us that was being filled with only the DJ's loud music. "You don't remember anything about the affair?"

The sip I am taking from my Virgin Mojito gets stuck in my throat.

Affair?

Did she say affair?

What affair?

Whose affair?

Is she referring to my affair with Ronit? Do they know about Ronit?

I realize that Koel and Shanaya are looking at me pointedly, waiting for my reply.

"Hey," a woman screams, as she suddenly appears out of nowhere and comes and hugs Koel and Shanaya, totally unaware of the explosive atmosphere at the table.

This must be Ayesha.

She is a tall woman with jet black hair, wearing a green, shimmery, ankle length, sleeveless one piece.

She has applied so much kohl around her eyes that they somehow look like they have big, dark black circles around them. Or maybe it's the effect of the lighting.

I stiffen when I think that she is about to hug me too, but she just goes around me, takes the fourth seat at the table, and gives me a cursory nod.

"Good to see you...after a long time," she says in a measured tone.

One thing I have realized in the few moments that I have been with these girls, is that our group hasn't broken. It's me who has been the outcast. They look like they are still the best of friends and regularly hang out. It's me who they don't include any longer.

"Did I miss something?" Ayesha questions, seeing our grave expressions.

"Mihika has forgotten everything that happened in the past six years," Koel recites like a poem.

Ayesha nods. Of course, Koel has told her this before.

I don't interject. I wait.

"So we were asking her if she has forgotten absolutely everything, or if she remembers the affair," she says.

Now three pairs of eyes are expectantly watching me and I have no idea what they are talking about.

"What affair?" I ask finally when I can find my voice from the deep recess my throat has suddenly turned into.

The three of them exchange knowing looks.

They look unconvinced that I don't remember it.

The waitress interrupts the tension at our table as she asks Ayesha what she would like to have.

Ayesha settles for a glass of white wine and orders chicken wings.

I begin thinking of how to strategically leave this failure of a meeting. They don't seem to be about to reveal anything to me. And their sole intention seems to be to humiliate and mock me, and if that is so, then I am done here.

"You never asked me why Ritu didn't come today," Koel says.

She is still looking at me with the same untrusting expression.

I shrug. If this is how they are going to treat me, I guess I don't even care anymore.

"I was just hoping you all could help me remember something from my past, since apparently we all were friends...," I begin, attempting to conclude this evening and take their leave.

A small preamble before making an abrupt exit.

"Well, we were indeed friends....till you had an affair with your best friend's husband," Koel says, a sharpness lining her tone.

"What?" I ask, my mouth aghast.

"Mohan. Ritu's husband," Shanaya clarifies.

I look from one to the other, utterly confused.

Are they telling me that I had an affair with my best friend's husband?

How could I do that? And why?

I don't know what convinces them more, my speechlessness or my utterly shocked expression, but they begin telling me more.

"We were, indeed, the best of friends. We used to hang out at least once a month, if not more often. But then Ritu found out you and Mohan were cheating on her. And of course, on poor Hrehan too. That was the day....we stopped seeing you," Shanaya says.

I don't get this. How could I have done such a thing?

And why?

What about Ronit?

He said we had become intimate.

So was I having an affair with him as well?

What the hell had been going on in my life?

Why would I cheat on my husband – a loving husband like Hrehan, and go in search of such activities outside?

I don't know what to say. When I think of it, if I were in their shoes, I would behave exactly like they do with me.

Because if what they are saying is true, I must have been a horrible person.

"Ritu has never forgiven you for what you did. Even when I told her you had forgotten everything. She was your closest friend. And you stabbed her in the back," Koel says.

I look up but Koel looks blurred because my eyes are brimmed with tears.

The music suddenly feels like it is suffocating me.

I close my eyes and put my fingers to my ears. My heart is beating so fast that I have to take long breaths to calm down.

"Will you like a refill, ladies?" the waitress asks again as she places Ayesha's order on the table.

Then she probably realizes we have hardly touched our drinks. The tension on our table is palpable now.

"We will call you if we need anything. Please stop interrupting us," Koel scowls at her.

"Sorry," the waitress mutters, her face reddening, and disappears.

So Koel is not being mean to just me. She is a mean person.

But right now, I have to focus on the reason I came here.

"Does...does Hrehan know?" I ask.

Koel shrugs. "Maybe. Maybe not. We never met you after that fallout. So we had no idea what was going on in your life till you messaged me on Facebook. We knew about the accident and your coma from the newspapers," she tells me.

I look down at the chicken wings. I have lost my appetite completely. I don't even want to finish my mocktail. I just want to go home, crawl underneath my duvet, clutch the pillow in my hands, press my face in it, and cry.

Another bout of heavy silence follows. I want to leave. But I guess I could get as much information out of these hostile girls while they are willing to share.

"Where did I meet Mohan?" I ask.

"Are you serious?" Shanaya laughs.

I ignore her.

"He works in your husband's company. Or used to work. He left the job after all this," Koel says, waving at me to indicate 'all this'.

I sigh. "How did Ritu find out?"

"She followed him once to see where he went on Sundays, claiming that he was going to play golf," Shanaya adds.

"And?"

"She caught you both red-handed at Hotel Lilian," Koel says.

"He had just lied about the sport he was playing," Shanaya says, and Koel and Shanaya burst out laughing.

My face burns with embarrassment and humiliation.

I look over at Ayesha who looks mortified too.

I stand up.

"I think I should leave," I say.

I don't even care about making any excuses anymore. I don't think I am going to meet these girls ever again. I don't even understand how I was friends with them at any point in time. They are the prodigal mean girls. Except Ayesha maybe.

Koel and Shanaya are shocked by my sudden stance. But they just look at me defiantly while I pick up my things.

No one tries to stop me. And I am thankful for that.

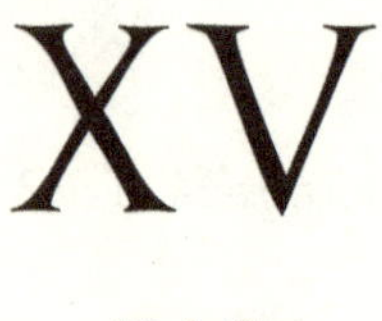

Back home, Hrehan is surprised I returned so early from the party.

"How was it?" he asks from the sofa where he is sitting with the laptop perched on his lap.

"I hated all of them. I can't believe they were my friends once upon a time," I say.

Hrehan laughs.

"You have changed," he says.

I look at him, puzzled.

"What do you mean?" I ask.

"I don't know. It's complicated to explain. After your head injury, it's like...like you are an altogether different person. You know what I mean? You just look like your old self. But your behaviour is completely different. Your personality...it has undergone a massive change," he says.

I am confused. I look like me but I don't behave like me? How is that even possible? I am still the same person, right?

"To be honest, I never liked the girls. They are snobbish and arrogant and harbour a major superiority complex. But you were like them. You enjoyed their company because you fit in," he says.

I ponder on his words. Was I really like them? Mean? Mean to friends? Mean to waiters?

But whatever it is, I definitely DO NOT fit in with them now!

And now I wonder whether I should tell Hrehan what I learnt tonight. I feel ashamed of what they say I have done.

But then, what will telling him achieve? I don't want to see the hurt in his eyes if it's news to him.

Anyway, that part is in the past. I don't even remember this Mohan. So, I will not broach the topic with Hrehan now.

Some skeletons are better buried inside a closet.

"I have ordered Italian food. Come, let's eat," Hrehan says, and I follow him to the dining room.

My cell phone pings as we are having dinner. I check the phone.

It's a text from an unknown number. I click it open.

'Hey. Ayesha here. I am sorry for the way things turned out tonight. I could see you were hurting and I didn't like the way those two handled the situation. If it helps you in any way, I will like to meet you and help you remember things from the past. Just let me know. Take care.'

At least Ayesha seems sensible.

'Thanks for your concern. I would love to meet you and talk to you. Good night,' I type back.

"By the way, I have forwarded the number plate details of that red car to Inspector Ashwin. He said he will check it out," Hrehan says.

"Okay," I reply with a slight relief. Hopefully tomorrow we will know who is following me and why.

*****

The next morning, I get ready with Hrehan. I am excited and scared at the same time to visit the place I used to work at before the accident.

I am suddenly conscious about my appearance. Should I look casual? Should I look formal?

Just like yesterday night, all pairs of eyes there will be on me, analyzing me, judging me.

Finally, I settle on a cream button-down shirt and a long brown ankle-length skirt. A mix of formal and casual.

I then apply just a bit of compact and nude lipstick. Just a touch of make-up, nothing too over the board.

"Ready?" Hrehan asks, smiling. "You look different," he adds.

"Really? How?" I ask.

He shrugs. "Just the way you dress, apply make-up, everything has changed," he says.

I don't remember how I used to dress or apply make-up when I went to the office.

"But I like this version of you better," he smiles.

I smile back, and we leave the house together.

Radha arrives just as we are getting in the car.

"You are going back to the office to work?" she asks in astonishment.

"No. Just a visit. She will be back soon," Hrehan replies for me.

As I sit inside, I wonder why Radha is so concerned about me joining the office back. Because most of the days, she doesn't speak a word to me. What is it that she wants from me or knows about me?

As we ride the car together in the back seat, I feel a small twinge of excitement.

"Nervous?" Hrehan asks, and places his hand over mine.

He squeezes my hand and suddenly, the world around me spins.

I am in a car, but in some alternate universe. I am wearing a brown, tight-fitting blouse and a pair of white trousers. I am laughing hard. I can feel the touch of a man's hand in mine as I laugh. I can hear him laugh too. I turn my neck to my right side to look at him. But it's not Hrehan sitting there. It's a man I have never seen before. He is the one who has his hand in mine, and he is the one I am laughing with.

And I scream.

"Mihika...Mihika...are you alright?" I hear Hrehan shout.

My throat feels dry, almost parched, and I am breathing heavily.

I open my eyes, scared the world around me will spin again, but it doesn't.

I focus my eyes on Hrehan who is holding me by my shoulders, looking at me with worry lining his eyes.

"Shall we go back home?" he asks.

"No," I say, taking deep breaths, "I am fine, I am fine, just a bit of dizziness," I say, steadying myself on my seat.

"Are you sure?" Hrehan asks.

He is looking at me unsure of what to do.

The driver slows down the car, watching me in the rear view mirror.

"Yes, yes," I reply.

Hrehan looks unconvinced, yet he doesn't persist about returning home.

I can't tell him what just happened. I just had another flashback. But I saw myself with another man. And it felt like I was too comfortable with him.

Was that Mohan?

Hrehan nods to the driver to continue, and he accelerates the car.

We stay silent the rest of the ride, me looking out of the windshield at the buildings and trees rushing past, and

Hrehan casting me sideways glances every few moments to make sure I am not about to have another episode.

We arrive at the huge campus of the Malik group of industries. The main building is made of a glass façade on the front, and sun rays reflecting from the wall illuminate the entire street across it.

I squint in the sun, shielding my eyes from the onslaught of the reflected light, to see how tall this building lurks above. It seems to be at least ten storeys.

I pause to see if the vision of this building triggers any memory. But I don't get any flashbacks.

"Shall we?" Hrehan asks, smiling.

I nod and follow Hrehan inside the plush entrance. I keep my eyes on the floor as I can sense many curious pairs of eyes watching me as we walk past the main reception area and board the elevator.

The interior is nothing short of a five-star hotel, and it seems tastefully and painstakingly decorated.

"My office is on the fifth floor, you worked on the fourth. I will take you to your department," Hrehan says.

"No. You proceed to your office. I will go on my own," I reply.

Hrehan looks at me with the same expression again – unsure of what to do.

"I will be fine, don't worry," I reassure him.

I alight on the fourth floor.

"You can call the driver and go home whenever you feel like," Hrehan tells me as the elevator doors close and I stand there, facing a full-length mirror, staring into my reflection.

"Mihika?" I turn around at the sweet voice to see a short, stout woman, roughly my age, with brownish hair set around her head in a bob cut, wearing a blue and white striped long kurta and dark blue jeans, smiling at me, a bunch of files in her hands.

"Oh. You don't remember me," she guesses, the smile vanishing from her face.

I then realize I have been staring at her without reciprocating her smile.

"Oh, I am sorry, but yes, I still haven't got my memory back," I say, wondering when I will have my next flashback now that I am at the place I used to work.

"I am Nisha, I used to be your accounting assistant," she says, smiling again.

"How are you doing now? It's so good to see you after such a long time," she gushes.

There are some people you develop an instant liking to, even though you have never met before (seemingly, in my case). Nisha is one of them. She has an easy smile and manner, and her body language reinforces an easy camaraderie.

"I am good, thanks. I just thought it would be good if I visited my workplace, just to get a hang of how my life was...before...," I linger.

"Oh, sure. Please follow me," she says.

I follow her down a long corridor to a section labeled 'Accounts department'.

We go in through the glass door. Inside, there is one desk and chair on the left side, with a desktop computer and intercom, and two cabins on the right side that share a wall.

The name on one cabin door reads 'Mrs. Mihika Malik, Accounting Manager 2', and the other one reads 'Mr. Mohan Verma, Accounting Manager 1'.

Mohan!

"So isn't anyone working in my place?" I ask.

Nisha shrugs.

"Hrehan sir has not appointed anyone to look into the accounts since you...you know...had the accident," she says.

I look at her. Nisha looks quite naïve. Like she will answer everything I ask her truthfully.

Does she know what happened between Mohan and me?

Well, at least she doesn't know that I know it now. For her, I have no memory at all.

So I decide to take a chance.

"Where is Mr. Mohan?" I ask.

"Umm, why don't we sit and talk?" she suggests, gesturing towards her desk.

I realize she has been fumbling with the files in her hands.

"Yes sure," I reply.

We walk the short distance to her desk and sit, me on the seat across hers.

"Actually, Mohan sir left some time back," she says then, after dumping the files in a cabinet and taking a seat.

"Why? What happened?" I ask, making sure my face shows the appropriate amount of curiosity.

"Well," she looks a little perplexed and overwhelmed, as if debating whether or not to tell me the truth.

I nod at her encouragingly.

"Actually," she says, probably deciding to confide in me, "there was a fallout between Mohan sir and Hrehan sir."

I swallow.

"What about?" I ask.

I brace myself to hear about my alleged affair with him.

"About some financial transactions," she says.

Financial transactions?

I am confused.

I thought it had been my affair with Mohan that resulted in him leaving the job.

"What happened exactly?" I ask.

Nisha is visibly restless now.

"Ma'am, I shouldn't be stressing you with all of this information..." she says, in a pleading tone.

"Please, Nisha. I have to know. What happened?" I persist.

"There were some...unaccountable transactions," she says.

"Means?"

"Money laundering. Or that is what Hrehan sir blamed him for."

Was Mohan involved in money laundering?

Was I onto him? Did our affair give me the upper hand in finding out about his misdemeanor?

Did I tell Hrehan about it?

Was Mohan behind my accident?

But we were having an affair!

Then did we break up because of this?

Was he the one who was after my life? Or Hrehan's?

Could he do that? Was he capable?

My brain has suddenly started racing at the speed of light.

I have to calm down. I can't just jump to conclusions. I need to get my facts right.

"Money laundering? How much?" I ask trying not to sound utterly desperate.

Nisha swallows.

"Almost twenty crores".

What!

"So did Mohan confess to it?"

I need to know if he confessed or if I found out about it.

"What? No! He swore he had no idea what happened to that money," she says.

"Then how did Hrehan come to know about it?" I question.

If I didn't catch him, how did he get caught?

Nisha shrugs. "I have no idea."

“So was that money recovered?” I ask.

“No. It has been transferred to some shell companies, details of which are not known. Hrehan sir has been trying to retrieve all of....”

"NISHA"!

Nisha's sentence is cut short by Hrehan's voice.

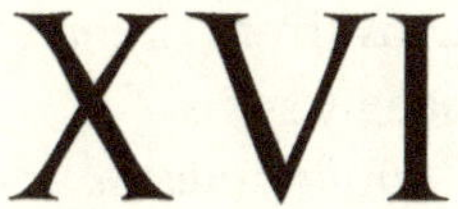

“Nisha. Mihika is still recovering. She is here just for a plain, simple visit. We are not supposed to stress her about anything,” Hrehan’s voice booms sternly down the hall as he approaches us with rapid footsteps. It’s a voice that I have never heard from him before.

Nisha stands up, sheepishly.

“S-sorry sir. Madam asked so...”

“Did you get those files?” he cuts her again.

“Y-yes,” she replies.

“Bring them to my cabin,” he orders her.

"Yes sir," Nisha says in a small voice.

I feel sorry for her for putting her in the spot.

“Mihika,” Hrehan turns to me, his voice suddenly soft. “Come to my cabin. I have something to tell you.”

I desperately wanted to know more about what Nisha had to tell me. But I see no way of that happening. So I oblige and follow Hrehan to his cabin on the fifth floor.

Hrehan’s office is a stark white office. It looks like it’s white washed. The walls are stark white, not a single blemish on them. The desk has a white marble top. The flooring is made up of white marbles.

I walk carefully, worried my soles will leave dust prints on the plush white flooring.

As I get seated across from Hrehan on the white leather chair, the world suddenly spins.

I am in another, parallel universe. It's the same room, and everything is the same.

Except this time, it's me sitting in Hrehan's chair, staring at me from across the desk.

I jerk back to the present to find Hrehan waving his hand in front of my eyes.

"Where are you lost?" He is asking.

I was lost in my past.

This flashback was very short, for just a fraction of a second.

But it was a strong memory.

I was clearly sitting in Hrehan's chair.

But why? What had I been doing?

"We should meet your neurologist once more," Hrehan is saying.

"You suddenly zone out, out of the blue. For a moment, you seem to be here, and the next, it's like you are lost, and in a trance. Your eyes lose focus and you stare unblinkingly across," he says.

Is that how I look when I am having a flashback?

I shake my head.

"I am fine," I say.

I can't have the neurologist prescribe me something that will stop me from getting these flashbacks. I need them. They are the only ray of hope I have for remembering everything I have forgotten.

And of course, Dr Veeksha's hypnotherapy tomorrow which I am looking forward to.

Nisha enters the room and places the bunch of files she was previously carrying onto the desk.

She doesn't look at me, and I feel guilty. But there is nothing I can say to her now. I will have to speak to her, but some other time.

"What did you want to tell me?" I ask as we hear Nisha's shoes click-clacking across the marble tiles as she recedes.

"You gave me the registration number of the red car that has been following you," he states, looking at me with his brows furrowed.

"Yes," I wait.

"I had forwarded those details to inspector Ashwin. He called back".

"What did he say?"

"He told me a shocking thing. The number plate of that car is the same number that belonged to the truck that hit you. The same number plate that has been missing since then," he says.

I am dumbfounded. Why would the number plate of the truck involved in my hit and run be the same as the number plate of the car that has been stalking me, unless....unless it was planned?

"That means...." I think loudly.

Hrehan nods gravely. "That means it confirms our theory that it was not an accident. It was an attempted murder," Hrehan says.

I gulp. Why and who could want me dead?

"And it means they still want to finish the job they started," I say, realization dawning on me.

The red car following me is stalking me so that it can mow me down whenever they get a chance!

Hrehan places his hand on mine, and it feels so warm, which makes me realise how cold my extremities have turned.

"Don't panic. The police have reopened the case. And since attempted murder is a serious allegation, they will try to trace that car before it goes off the radar. That is what Ashwin has promised me," Hrehan says, sensing the dread forming in my mind.

I don't know what to think, what to make of all this.

"Hrehan," I say, "Can I ask you something? Will you reply honestly?"

"Of course," he says, squeezing my hand.

"Have I done anything bad in these past years? Anything that would make someone want to kill me?"

Hrehan doesn't reply immediately. He looks down at our interlocked hands, his lips pressed into a thin line.

Does he know something and is considering whether or not to tell me about it?

"Well, you may have done some bad things, but I wouldn't say they justify wanting to kill you," he gives me a diplomatic answer. An answer that is neither honest nor dishonest.

"Nisha was telling me about the financial..."

Hrehan cuts me off, squeezing my hand once more.

"Ignore Nisha. You need not worry about that. I have things under control here. What we should focus on is your mental recovery, physical recovery, and catching the culprits who made an attempt on your life. Stop worrying about other things. I am here. I will take care of everything."

Despite his reassurance, I don't feel good at all.

I desperately need to know what I have done, and why there are people after my life!

I can't just sit and rest while the world around me makes no sense at all!

But Hrehan neither tells me anything more, nor does he entertain any more questions. He tells me I need to go back home, take my afternoon medicines, have lunch, and rest.

On our way out, I notice a woman sitting at the secretary's desk outside Hrehan's office. The woman is stout, with greying hair, probably in her late fifties.

I stop in my tracks. Didn't Ronit tell me that I suspected Hrehan of having an affair with a woman called Anaisha? My husband's secretary?

I keep staring at the woman who is struggling to type something on the desktop in front of her, her eyes crinkling behind her soda bottle glasses.

"What happened?" Hrehan asks me.

At that, the woman looks up from her computer and smiles when she sees me. She is missing one front incisor.

"Nothing. You go back to work. I will leave on my own. Don't worry about me," I tell Hrehan.

"No, I will escort you," he insists.

"You don't have to. If that makes you feel any better, let your secretary escort me. Won't you?" I ask the lady.

"Sure, why not?" she smiles, flashing her one-tooth-less smile, adjusting her glasses on her flat nose, wiggling out of the chair she was stuck into.

Hrehan sighs. "You always have your way," he smiles at me.

"Please escort madam to the car," he tells the woman who nods.

She looks happy to escort me, rather than doing whatever she was struggling to do.

"Hi, I am Mihika," I tell her, wanting to make her feel comfortable before I begin my interrogation, as we walk slowly down the corridor.

"I am Mrs. Fernandez," she smiles. "I know you, and what happened to you. It...it must have been terrible," she adds.

"Yes. The worst part is the memory loss. I don't remember the last six years of my life," I tell her as we board the elevator.

"Oh, that must be awful," she says, as the elevator doors close and we begin descending.

"It is. So we must have met before, right? Even if I don't remember it?" I ask, sounding as casual as I can.

"No ma'am. I joined just after your...accident," she says.

"Oh. Then who was working with Hrehan before you?" I ask innocently.

The elevator doors open and we step outside.

Mrs. Fernandez casts a conspiratorial glance around us to make sure no one is eavesdropping.

"Some pretty young chick. I don't know her name. But she had created a scandal it seems. She was fired," she whispers, her eyes so big that they bulge out of their sockets.

"Scandal?" I ask.

Is she referring to her affair with Hrehan? If indeed it was true?

Mrs. Fernandez again looks around us, and after confirming that no one is giving us a second glance, she whispers again.

"She had filed a complaint of sexual harassment against Mr. Hrehan".

"What?" I ask, shocked.

"No, no. Don't doubt your husband for even one second. He was innocent. She tried to blackmail him for something he never did, to earn some easy money. But an internal inquiry was set up, and she was found guilty of fake charges. She is lucky Hrehan sir didn't drag her to court.

I am happy they hired me in her place. They need sincere, hardworking people for that position. Not characterless girls who are after money and nothing else..."

I have zoned out of Mrs. Fernandez's monologue by the time we reach the car.

"Thank you so much for escorting me," I tell her, thankful that I have time to myself now, after listening to what she has told me.

I need time to think, to ponder over what I just heard.

"Any time. It was nice to meet you finally ma'am, do come again," she tells me, patting my shoulder in a motherly gesture.

As the car rides fast on the highway, my mind won't stop twirling.

One thing is confirmed. Ronit hasn't told me all lies. There is some truth to what he said.

But whatever I am discovering, is twisted from the facts he told me.

He told me things about Hrehan, which were only partially true. They didn't represent the entire truth.

He told me Hrehan hid the fact that I was working at his firm before my accident because he is a possessive, physically abusive husband who wanted to control me. But even though the truth remained that Hrehan had indeed hidden it from me, his reasons were entirely different. It was done out of love and care for me.

I have now been with Hrehan for more than a month, and never have I experienced anything with him that can describe him as a possessive, manipulative, or emotionally and physically abusive husband!

The same thing is true about Anaisha and her alleged affair with Hrehan. Today I learnt a totally different perspective about that.

But how would Ronit know about it unless it was indeed me who gave him that information?

And if what Mrs. Fernandez told me is the truth, and if Anaisha was just blackmailing Hrehan for money without any base, why did I hire Ronit to investigate Hrehan's affair with her?

Coming to think of it, he had said we never found any substantial proof about the affair, but there were circumstantial pieces of evidence. What did he mean by that?

My mind is going bonkers and I can feel the beginnings of an oncoming headache across my temples.

Radha asks me if I want to have lunch as soon as I reach home. But food is the last thing on my mind.

I tell her to finish her work and go home, and that I will eat later.

I climb the stairs and notice that she is still lingering at the bottom of the staircase.

"What?" I ask her.

Her staring is now bordering on creepiness.

"How was it?" she asks, looking at me pointedly.

"How was what?" I ask.

"Visit to the office? Did you remember anything at all?"

I squint my eyes trying to understand this woman.

Why does she desperately want me to remember my past? What is it to her?

"Is there something specific you want me to remember Radha?" I question in a stern voice.

She keeps staring at me for a few minutes unabashedly.

We are almost having a who-blinks-first match when she turns around, mutters something akin to 'never mind,' and disappears inside the kitchen.

I throw my hands up in the air in frustration.

To add to everything that's going around me and driving me crazy, there is Radha who I just can't figure out.

I pace in my room, feeling restless.

The more I try to find answers, the more questions get raised.

It feels like I am walking into a labyrinth. The more I try to find a way out, the more I go into its depths.

Finally, I take a paper pad from the desk and a pen and sit down on the bed.

I decide to start by writing down everything I have learnt so far.

I want to have everything in front of me. Only then, probably, I will be able to connect the dots.

I begin writing.

1. Nikhil is dead. His colleague Ritika won't speak to me. Nikhil died in Jan 2018. He had posted depressing quotes on Facebook starting from July 2017. I know all was well between us till March 2017. So question no. 1, when did we break up? No. 2, why? And number 3, how did he die?

2. I married Hrehan in February 2018. We met in my advertising firm and we were married within a year of meeting. So, I had probably broken up with Nikhil by then. I try to work out the time frame. Hrehan said we married around 9 months after I met him for the first time. That means we met in June 2017. That means Nikhil and I broke up sometime between March and May 2017? Does that make any sense? What could have caused us to break up, with me hooking up with a new man so quickly? Didn't I feel the heartache of the breakup?

3. I had an affair with Ronit. According to Ronit, I hired him almost a year ago, to investigate Hrehan because I suspected he was having an affair with Anaisha, his secretary. We did find some circumstantial evidence about

the same, but no hard proof. Now today I learnt that Anaisha made fake sexual harassment charges against Hrehan to blackmail him and extract money, but an internal inquiry committee cleared him and she was fired from the job.

4. Ronit also told me that I was planning to leave Hrehan because I was not happy in the marriage. Hrehan was an abusive and controlling husband who kept tabs on me at all times and who I wanted to escape.

5. My friendship with my girlfriends went sour after I had an affair with the husband of my best friend Ritu – Mohan, who also happened to be my colleague at work. This also happened about a year back. But that's not all. Mohan was involved in some illegal financial fraud at the company for which he was fired by Hrehan, and now, Hrehan looks after all the accounting work himself. He hasn't replaced either me or Mohan. Why?

6. Six months back, at 2 AM at the intersection in front of City Mall, a truck hit me resulting in a six-month-long coma. Now we know that this was not an accident, but an attempted murder, and the same person who was driving the truck is now stalking me in a red car. Why?

7. And last but not least, Radha. Why does she stare at me the way she does? I always get the feeling that she knows something and she keeps looking at me hoping that I will remember something. What is it? She closes up every time I try to dig into it, but once she did say something. When I stealthily went to meet Ronit in an auto, she told me I used to do that often before. And she also asked me whether she should call 'him'. Who is the man she was referring to? She looked excited when she thought I was going back to work. Why is she waiting so desperately for me to get my memory back?

I decide I will go step by step and figure out what each of these leads mean, and how I can investigate more.

Somehow all these facts feel like the lost pieces of a single big puzzle. I just need to sit down and try to fit the pieces amongst themselves and with each other.

My phone pings.

It's Yana. From Yoga class.

'Hey. How are you? Want to go for a coffee?' her text reads.

I guess I need to take my mind away from all of this.

'Sure. Where can we meet?' I reply.

'Come to Café Supreme on RN Road'.

'See you soon,' I type back, making a mental note to ask her everything she can remember about my life back then.

I decide to go by auto as I don't want to draw anyone's attention. If Hrehan is keeping tabs on me, I don't want him to know who I am hanging out with. If the red car is following my car, I don't want to lead it.

I reach Café Supreme fifteen minutes later. My mind is still bubbling with innumerable questions, when I spot Yana waving at me from a table at the far corner.

I smile back at her and join her at the table. A perky young waitress approaches us promptly.

We order two cappuccinos and a black forest pastry. I am still unsure why Yana called me—if she has something specific to share or if it's just because she felt like reviving our long-lost friendship. "So, what's up? How are you doing?" she asks.

I shrug. "The same old. I haven't been able to figure out what I was up to the past six years," I say, trying to humour her.

She gives me an understanding smile.

"We used to meet here, you know, before...," she says.

"Oh," I reply.

The cappuccinos arrive. This feels a little awkward. I don't know how close I was to Yana back when I used to go to Yoga classes. But right now, I have absolutely no memory of her. I know nothing about her. So, I don't know what exactly to talk to her about other than my own issues.

"So, how's the office?" she asks me out of the blue.

I look at her, a question mark on my face. How the hell does she know I went to my workplace?

"How do you know I went to my office?" I ask her.

For just a fraction of a second, her expression falters, as if she has unveiled something. But then, she smiles instantly.

"Well, knowing you, you would never sit at home doing nothing. You were bound to join back, sooner than later, aren't I right?" she says, smiling.

I wait a beat before replying.

"I just went to get a feel of things, to feel normal. The doctors still feel I need to stay out of stressful situations and need neurological monitoring. So I am not sure when I will be able to actually join back," I say.

"Oh! So anyway, how are things there? Now?"

It's the way she says 'Now' that catches me. And the way she is staring at me.

This is not a casual question.

I put the mug that I had almost touched my lips down, back on the table.

"What do you mean by '*Now*'?" I ask her.

She shrugs, trying to appear nonchalant.

"There were problems...before," she says.

I know there were problems. But why would I tell them to Yana? Was she so close to me?

"What problems?" I ask.

She looks down at her mug thoughtfully, as if the light brown liquid inside holds the answers to everything. Then she looks up.

“You were having problems with your husband,” she says.

“Did I tell you that?” I ask.

“Yes. You were troubled. He was emotionally and physically abusive. He used to hit you often. He used to control you. He was also unfaithful. In fact, when I first heard about the accident, I wondered if it was not an accident, but a...,” she leaves her sentence hanging.

I am stunned. She is telling me exactly what Ronit has told me before, but something that I have found difficult to believe, considering Hrehan’s current behaviour.

But how would she know so many things about me, my life, my workplace, my husband, unless I told them to her?

What else does she know? What else have I shared with her?

"Does he...does he hit you even now?" She asks softly, her eyes creased at the angles with worry.

I shake my head.

"No. In fact, he has been so loving and caring towards me since I woke up from the accident, that it is difficult to believe what you are telling me," I tell her the truth.

"I bet," she says with a smirk.

"What do you mean?" I ask.

She looks down at her mug again, and then glances back up at me.

"Do you remember anything that happened at your workplace?" she asks.

I shake my head. She is looking at me pointedly, and I steel myself to listen to what she has to tell me.

She takes a good look at me and then shakes her head.

"Actually, I am not sure I should be telling you all this. You are still recovering from a neurological injury and..."

"Please, Yana, for the sake of my mental peace, I need to know what has happened in the time I was blacked out. I will go crazy if I don't understand. If we were good friends, please patronize me," I beg her.

She sighs.

"Hrehan was committing a financial fraud. Under the guise of donating to charity, he was embezzling funds from the company accounts," she says.

What?

Till now, I was under the impression that it was Mohan who was committing the fraud.

"Why?" I ask.

I don't understand. Why would Hrehan steal from his own company?

"The company was running at a loss. To make an impression on the stakeholders that all was well, the company was shown to be afloat by taking loans from foreign banks," she says.

"What?"

I don't understand. How is this possible?

Every person I meet tells me a version of the truth. And each version is different from the other. What is the real truth?

"Hrehan planned to steal the remaining money from the company by embezzling the funds to some offshore untraceable account, and then vanish," she says. "He probably planned to elope with his lover. Wait, you know about his lover, right?" she asks. She probably realizes that I may not be aware of it.

But I nod. "I have some idea," I reply.

"Oh, Thank God. I wouldn't want to be the first person to tell you about it. Your husband was cheating on you with his secretary, Anaisha," she says.

I just nod. I know another version of this truth, but I decide to just listen to what Yana has to say.

"Anyway, you found out about everything. You discovered the financial fraud. You found out he was cheating on you. And all of Hrehan's plans collapsed," she adds.

I listen in rapt attention as she goes ahead.

"Amidst all of this, the only good thing for you was, to reduce his own losses, Hrehan made you a significant stakeholder in the company. His idea was to have you bear the brunt of all the losses as well as the angst of other stakeholders once the company started drowning."

"But when you found out, you stopped the money from leaving the company without your supervision. You also traced the bank from where the loan was issued and started paying it off in small installments."

"You had confided in me. You had told me that you felt your life was in danger because you knew Hrehan could go to any limits to get what he wanted. So I think, with his fraud on the verge of exposure, Hrehan made a new plan. A plan to eliminate you. Because you knew too much. And because he was your nominee. So if you conveniently died in an accident, his fraud would never get caught, and he would still be the maximum stakeholder in the company," she says.

A chill runs down my spine. What is she trying to say? That Hrehan tried to kill me?

Yana smiles at me patronizingly.

I am too dumbfounded to respond.

So is this all a part of the master plan orchestrated by Hrehan?

If this is indeed true, Hrehan is one hell of an actor!

But the more I listen to Yana, the more I believe it. She can't fabricate to this extent.

And everything perfectly fits in if what she says is true. It also explains why Hrehan is behaving in such a loving way with me. If he indeed tried to get rid of me, and yet I survived, then two things are true. One, since I can't remember anything, he doesn't have to fear I would expose his financial fraud. That also explains why he fired Mohan, who was probably also in on all of this, and it also explains why he is handling all the finances without hiring any help to replace me or Mohan. That way, he is covering his tracks. He might even be slowly recovering the money so that the fraud might never be exposed.

Second, as Yana says, if I am the maximum stakeholder, with me being his wife and he being my nominee, he still holds the maximum stakes in the company. I have no idea who the other stakeholders are and what their role is in all of this, but that is something I have to find out.

"Are you ok?" Yana pulls me out of my trance, waving one hand before me.

"Yeah, sorry," I reply, drinking my coffee, which has turned cold by now, in one swift go.

"That was why I was asking you how things were at work," she says.

I nod. The need to go to the office, to my work desk, my computer, the financial details, and the files feels overwhelming. I have to check everything to understand what truly happened.

As if she's been reading my mind, "here," Yana says, removing something from her purse. I watch as she places a key card on my table.

The card has my photo and the logo of Malik Industries on it.

I look at her, confused.

"This is your duplicate office card. You had kept a copy with me just in case. I guess you might need it now," she says.

I take the card and look at my photograph, staring back at me.

Yet, as I look into those eyes, it feels like I am looking at a stranger.

XVIII

The next morning, I stand outside Dr. Bhatnagar's consulting room, my heart beating in trepidation. I have already signed the consent form for the hypnotherapy session, and I am waiting for Dr Veeksha.

A patient exits her office, and Dr. Veeksha Bhatnagar comes out to greet me.

"Good morning Mihika. How are you?" she smiles from behind her gold-rimmed spectacles.

She looks fresh in a crisp beige-coloured starched cotton saree with colourful peacocks embroidered along its border.

"Good morning. I am good," I say, smiling a weak smile.

Even I can sense how hollow my words feel.

Dr. Veeksha senses my hesitation.

"Don't worry. Hypnotherapy will help you seek your answers," she says, guiding me towards a corridor that runs along the east wing of the building.

The corridor leads to a big black door at the dead end, and Dr. Veeksha uses her I-card to swipe at the door. With an eerie feeling refusing to leave the back of my mind, I enter inside.

The room is huge, with a high ceiling, as if they have merged two floors into one. A huge chandelier rests at the center of the ceiling, twinkling with bright yellow lights. The walls are painted in hues of only green – all shades of green – dark green, bottle green, light green, moss green, fluorescent green!

A relaxing couch rests at the center of the room, and an armchair is beside it.

Other than the two chairs, the room has absolutely no furniture.

"Please take a seat," Dr. Veeksha says, indicating the couch.

I swallow. I don't know what is going to happen next and the uncertainty that looms over is making me nervous.

Dr. Veeksha senses my thoughts, probably. She must be used to this kind of hesitation from her first-time patients.

I walk over to the brown leather couch and sit on it.

"Sit back and relax. The more relaxed your body is, the more relaxed your mind will be," Dr.Veeksha says as she takes a seat on the armchair.

I follow her instructions. I lie down on the couch, head resting on one arm which has a pillow to rest the head.

"Let me tell you some rules. Hypnotherapy sessions can be a bit harrowing. And while they can help you make progress when done in the right way, they can also prove dangerous if not done properly. Hence I want you to trust me completely. I will take you back to the memories that have been buried somewhere deep in your subconscious. But at any point, if I feel that these memories are triggering you, or causing any kind of adverse effects on your body, then we will have to withdraw irrespective of where we have reached. You must follow my voice and every word I say, and obey every command. Because if you lose my voice, it will be difficult for me to get you back, and this can turn into a medical emergency. You understand and agree to proceed?"

I nod. I have come too far to go back now. And I really don't care anymore. I just want my memories back, that's it!

"I will also be recording your session. Because many times patients do not remember whatever they have recollected in the hypnotherapy sessions. So they like to listen to it once they are done."

"Ok," I reply, bracing myself.

"Ready?"

"Yes," I say with a valour I don't feel.

"Close your eyes," Dr. Veeksha instructs.

There is something about this room. Maybe it's the soundproof walls and the cut-off from the outer environment that add an echoing quality to Dr. Veeksha's voice, and suddenly, here, her voice sounds hypnotic.

"Relax. Relax your body and mind. Concentrate only on my words, nothing else. Just follow what I am saying." And I give in to the situation. I follow every word Dr Veeksha says as she goes on.

"Concentrate on your breaths. Focus on every inhalation and exhalation. Inhale and exhale with me. With every inhale, feel your memory, the memory you have lost, come back to you. And with every exhale, feel the exhaustion from your brain going out of your body, leaving you forever. Breathe slow, breathe deep. Continue slow and deep breathing as we progress."

As the session progresses, I feel my mind and body completely relaxed as I cling to only one thing in this entire world – Dr. Veeksha's voice.

She has taken me back to the last thing I remember.

"What do you see?" She asks.

For a moment, I feel as if I have choked. I can't get the words out of my mouth.

Then suddenly my voice is free.

"I see Nikhil. He is watching the television. I am sitting at the dining table, working on my laptop."

"How do you feel?"

"I feel...angry."

"Why do you feel angry?"

"Nikhil just let go of an opportunity at promotion. A promotion that meant a higher salary, and a better life".

"Why did he refuse that opportunity?"

"It's in Delhi. He doesn't want to shift".

"Why not?"

"Because he wants to be near me. He doesn't want a long-distance relationship."

"And why aren't you happy with his decision?"

"I want to have more money in my life. I want success. I have many dreams. And being rich is one way of getting there."

"What is happening now?"

"My cell phone chimed."

"Who is it?"

I am silent.

"Who is it, Mihika?"

"It's Hrehan".

"What does the message say?"

"Thanks for the wonderful evening. Looking forward to seeing you again."

"What did you reply?"

I am silent.

"What did you reply, Mihika?"

"A heart emoji".

"Ok. Now I want you to fast forward one month ahead."

"Where are you now?'

"Mihika?"

"Please reply?"

"On the count of three, you will come back.

Three.

Two

One."

I jerk awake and sit up.

My forehead is filled with beads of sweat. I am hyperventilating and I can feel my heart thudding against my rib cage.

Dr. Veeksha hands me a glass of water.

I gulp the water in one go. Dr. Veeksha hands me a tissue to wipe my forehead.

"What happened? What did you see?" Dr. Veeksha asks me after I am slightly settled.

I shake my head. "I don't remember," I lie.

Dr. Veeksha nods.

"Do you remember the other things you saw?"

"Yes," I reply.

I am feeling suffocated here. I need to get out and breathe fresh air.

"It's okay to feel like this. Not every hypnotherapy session is going to be rosy. But at least you will remember some things," Dr. Veeksha says.

"Can we...can we go back to a specific point in time in these last six years?" I ask.

"Yes, we can try," she says.

"Can we do it now?" I ask, now desperate for answers.

Dr. Veeksha laughs.

"Don't be so impatient Mihika. You can't stress your body and mind out like this. We can't do it now, especially after the way you got triggered. This is not a magic wand that will get all of your memories back in one go. This is a slow process. And the slower we go, the better are your chances at retrieving all of your memories," she says.

I nod. I have only been half-listening. I lost her when she said no to another session right now. Because I am extremely disturbed by what I just saw.

Dr. Veeksha, on my insistence, schedules the next session for tomorrow.

Back home, I am feeling restless.

Finally, I open my laptop and google Nikhil's name.

Till now, I have searched for Nikhil on Facebook and tried to find out more about the circumstances around his death. But I never considered searching on Google because why would it make big news? But now I have a hunch that it had. And I am right.

As I search for 'Nikhil Gaur death Pune', I get multiple hits, the first article heading in capitals declaring ***'Pune techie commits suicide'***.

I feel a big lump forming in my throat as I read on.

'Nikhil Gaur, 28, a techie working with Infosys, Pune, committed suicide by hanging. He was found hanging at his flat by his neighbours who broke into the flat with the help of local police after the maid reported that Mr. Nikhil had not been responding for two days.

Neighbours describe him as a very sociable person who was actively involved in society gatherings and festivals. His work colleagues expressed shock over his untimely demise, claiming him to be a very sincere and hardworking person. No suicide note has been found, but speculation is that he was recently left heartbroken after his live-in partner of three years had cheated on him, and he had gone through a bad breakup.

His work colleague and best friend, Ritika Bhaskar, through tears, claimed that he died of heartache and that his ex-

girlfriend should be arrested for abetment of suicide. The police refused to comment on any of this.

He leaves behind a family consisting of a father, who is a retired army personnel, a mother, and a younger sister. The family stays at Ratnagiri, and has been informed.'

I sit back, my mind numb. This corroborates with what I saw in the hypnotherapy session.

The thing that triggered me, and disturbed me to the core.

I saw myself in bed with Hrehan, ignoring my mobile that kept vibrating with multiple incoming calls from Nikhil.

XIX

I pace our bedroom, feeling restless by the minute.

There is no doubt now in my mind, that while Nikhil was loyal to me, and even gave up an opportunity that paid him better just to be closer to me, I was the one who cheated on him, destroyed him, and probably drove him to suicide. I was the one who valued money more than people, more than meaningful relationships.

Why else would I ever cheat on him? I know how much he loved me, and I still believe I loved him back as fiercely. But could the greed and lust for more money and glamour make me do what I did? How could I have done such a cruel and terrible thing?

It's unfathomable!

But just remembering this won't serve any purpose. Nor will it bring Nikhil back.

A lot of unfathomable things have happened since then.

My alleged affair with Ronit.

My alleged affair with Mohan.

The embezzlement of funds.

And the attempt on my life.

If I want to understand all of this, I can't get emotional about something I have done in the past, which I have no recollection of anymore.

I will grieve Nikhil once I get through all of this.

I suddenly remember something.

I grab my mobile and open my old email ID.

mihikaflower@gmail.com.

I remember trying to open this one back when I got the smartphone. But I obviously didn't remember the password.

The hint question had been, the name of my boyfriend.

I had tried answering with Hrehan and Nikhil's names. But both were wrong.

Now I type 'Mohan' as the answer. It's wrong.

Then I type 'Ronit'.

And my email account opens.

I scroll down through my emails, scanning them to see if anything rings a bell.

Around 8 to 9 months back, there is an email from an '*anaisha999@gmail.com*'.

Anaisha? Hrehan's secretary? With whom he was supposedly having an affair, and to investigate whom I had first hired Ronit? The one who tried to blackmail Hrehan for sexual harassment?

Why had she been emailing me?

I open her email. There's a string of emails, spanning 3 to 4 months.

I open the last one from her.

To : mihikaflower@gmail.com

From : anaisha999@gmail.com

Subject : I want my money!!

Ma'am, I did everything you asked me to do, but you have not kept your end of the promise. Instead, I was fired from the job! I trusted you and have waited long enough. I know everything you have done. If I don't get the money you promised me in the next two days, I am turning you and everyone in. Love, Anaisha.

Stunned, I check the reply that I have sent to this last one.

To : anaisha999@gmail.com

From: mihikaflower@gmail.com

Subject : Your payment

I have told you not to contact me. This is the last correspondence between us. I am sending you the money. Henceforth, I want you to keep your mouth shut. And please, do not ever show your bloody face again. Below as an attachment is the screenshot of the money transaction.

As I open the attachment, I can see the screenshot of Rs. 2.5 lacs credited from some account to Anaisha's account.

I sit back, speechless. What I am reading, indicates only one thing.

Anaisha was not having an affair with Hrehan. She was only following my instructions. I was paying her off for doing the job. And it was me who she had been blackmailing!

But I don't understand. First, why did I plant Anaisha to make harassment charges against Hrehan? And if I indeed did that, why would I hire Ronit to look into their affair, when it was something created by me, for whatever reasons?

Something doesn't add up.

Is Ronit being truthful to me? Or is he too hiding facts?

On the spur of the moment, I decide to take a chance and reply to Anaisha's last email.

To : anaisha999@gmail.com

From: mihikaflower@gmail.com

Subject : Urgent

Hello Anaisha, I hope you are doing well. I need some help, and I think only you can help me right now. Please contact me on 986778990 as soon as possible. I am looking forward to speaking to you.

Yours sincerely,

Mihika Malik.

I hit send, biting my lip. I just hope she responds.

Looking at the last email that I sent her, it seems highly unlikely. But it is worth a shot.

That evening, I am a nervous wreck by the time Hrehan comes home.

It has been absolutely impossible for me to sit and do nothing when still so many pieces of the puzzle of my life are missing and the empty spaces are staring at me, teasing me, challenging me, and making me restless.

I haven't heard from Anaisha yet. And I have no idea if she is ever going to contact me.

"How was your hypnotherapy session?" Hrehan asks.

"Umm...good," I reply, not knowing what to say.

I still can't believe Hrehan can be a cruel mastermind manipulator the way Yana and Ronit have portrayed him, because the way he speaks to me and looks at me, tells me a different story.

I don't know what to think anymore. I don't know what to believe anymore.

But I have given it a thought.

If Hrehan really is the villain who has been after money, why would he encourage me to visit a psychologist and take hypnotherapy sessions when getting my memory back could be hazardous for him? Something just doesn't add up. And tonight, I am going to find out what.

"You seem distracted," Hrehan muses, pouring some red wine into his flute, eyeing me curiously.

"All okay? Did you recollect anything?"

I clear my throat.

"I did see some of the past events that I had forgotten about," I say.

"Which ones?" he asks, sitting down on the sofa.

"I saw Nikhil, my ex-fiance," I say.

"Oh," he exclaims, "Is he real?"

"What do you mean?" I ask, intrigued at his weird choice of words.

Hrehan shrugs.

"When we first met, you never mentioned any Nikhil. Never in all the five years of our marriage did you ever mention him. And since you woke up from the coma, he is all you have been asking about. I had discussed this with your neurologist and we had thought it could be a figment of your imagination. Brain injuries can do that to you sometimes. They are called confabulations. When your brain can't remember something, to fill in those memory gaps, it creates its own memory, an imaginary one. So we thought, Nikhil never existed in reality," he says.

I smile. Anything else can be imaginary. But Nikhil is – was – as real as me.

"Anyway, I am feeling really tired. I am going to call it a night," I say.

"Okay, what about dinner?" Hrehan asks.

"I don't have any appetite. Yours is ready on the dining table," I say and proceed towards my bedroom, clutching the duplicate I-card in my hand.

Now I just need to wait for Hrehan to fall asleep, so that I can go to the office and sneak inside. I need to find out what exactly happened.

In my bedroom, I dial Radha's number.

"Yes madam," she asks, sounding surprised that I am calling her at this time.

"Radha, you had said you could call someone to drop me?" I ask, remembering that puzzling conversation I had with her back when I was planning to take an auto to go and meet Ronit.

"You...you remember everything?" she asks.

"No. But I need your help. Tell me who used to drop me off whenever I did not want to take the car before."

There is a momentary hesitation before she says, "Naresh. My husband. He drives an auto. He used to drop you".

I have many questions for her but this is not the right time to ask.

"Send him here tonight. I need to go somewhere at midnight," I tell her.

"M...Madam, are you alright?" she asks, sounding unsure.

"Yes, don't worry, I will pay you," I say, thinking that that is what she is worried about.

"Pay...everything? Everything you promised before?"

What is she saying? What have I promised her before?

"I am talking about tonight. Rest of the things we will talk about later," I tell her.

"Ok. He will be there. I will forward you his contact number," she says.

"Thanks".

Night falls and I feel as awake as an owl as I listen to the rhythmic strokes of the wall clock.

Tick-tick-tick-tick.

At fifteen past midnight, clutching the I-card in my hands, I slowly open the door.

The house is dark and silent. The door to the guest bedroom is closed. Hrehan must be fast asleep by now. I tiptoe down the stairs, taking care not to make any noise.

I slowly open the latch on the main door, and close it as softly as I can behind me.

Sure enough, an auto is waiting for me at the end of the lane.

I half walk, and half run the short distance. I quickly sit in the passenger seat.

"Naresh?" I ask the man in the driver's seat.

He turns around to look at me and suddenly the world spins.

I am in a parallel universe, standing next to the auto, with the same man in the driver's seat. It is daytime.

"Do not come here from tomorrow. We won't need you any longer," I say.

"What about our money madam?" he asks.

"Don't you understand a word, you dimwit? I told you, I am soon going to get a lot of money. Then I will pay you. Then you and Radha can go and do whatever in that hell hole of yours, and stop bothering me forever," I say.

"Madam...madam, are you alright?"

I jerk awake as the man sprinkles some water on my face.

He is the same man I saw in the flashback.

I was so rude to him! And I had promised them money!

Is that the reason why Radha keeps asking me whether or not I have my memory back?

"I am okay. Can you please take me to the office?" I ask.

The man looks at me with a weird expression on his face.

"What happened?" I ask.

"You never talk like this to us madam. Radha did say you have changed," he says.

"What do you mean?"

"Nothing," he says, and starts the auto.

Twenty minutes later, we reach the office building.

"Take the small lane on the left and I will alight on the back side of the building," I tell him.

I am sure there will be a night security guard at the front door, who probably won't stop me from going inside, but will definitely recognize me. There might be CCTV cameras as well. But nobody would be watching them continuously. And till I know anything more, I don't want anyone to know what I am doing.

"You park in the corner. I will come back here, in the same place. If there is any change of plan, I will message or call you," I tell Naresh as I alight the auto.

"Okay madam," he replies dutifully and proceeds to park in a dark corner.

I walk along the fence. The alley is dark with a dilapidated building on the other side of the office and no street lights. It's eerily quiet too.

I keep my flashlight on. I am trying to see where I can climb the compound wall when I see a small opening in the fence. It's like a trapdoor.

It seems locked, but when I kick it, it opens.

I bend down, crawl inside through it, and pull the gate closed behind me, just as it had been.

Then I tiptoe around the office building, finding my way to the front.

The security guard is sitting in his cabin, watching some movie in a very loud volume.

Thankfully, the noise drowns down the sound my footsteps make.

I quickly walk to the front door, and swipe the card Yana gave me at the door, my eyes trained on the security guard the entire time.

As the door opens with a small creak, he looks up.

I freeze in my tracks. If he turns around, I am in plain sight. My legs feel paralyzed and just refuse to move.

But the security guard gives a loud sneeze and then, rubbing his nose with the back of his hand, goes back to watching his movie.

I heave a sigh of relief as I squeeze in through the door, my heart thumping in trepidation. I hope he can't hear my heartbeats because they sound like drums to my ears.

I stealthily close the door behind me.

Using my flashlight to illuminate my way, I quickly walk to the elevator. I reach the fourth floor and walk to the accounts department, and then to my cabin.

All doors are closed, but they open with the swipe of my duplicate I-card.

Once safely inside my cabin, I switch on the lights.

I know this cabin is at the backside of the building, so the security guard won't be able to see the lights on. And I don't think he is checking the CCTV at all, as the movie he is watching seems far more interesting to him.

I sit at my desk, switch on my computer, and wait while it boots.

Two minutes later, which seems like two hours, I see my home page. But it is password-protected.

Does Hrehan use my computer, I wonder.

The time it took to boot makes me think that it has been accessed after a really long time.

Or maybe Hrehan has changed the password?

I decide to try my luck.

I start with Nikhil's name, then Hrehan's name. Then Mohan. Then Ronit.

No luck.

Then I enter Hrehan's birthdate. Then mine.

Still no luck.

Then I enter our anniversary date.

Nothing.

I sit back, trying to think of what the password could be.

I am now almost sure that the password must have been changed by Hrehan. What would he set?

I enter my name – Mihikamalik.

Nothing happens.

Then randomly, I type Hrehanmihika.

And the homepage appears.

I heave another sigh of relief. This seems like a password reset by Hrehan. It seems too cringe for my taste. And given my promiscuous behaviour in the past, I don't see my past self keeping this password.

Anyway, one more hurdle crossed. I stare at the screen.

There are multiple folders on the desktop, and I open the one labeled 'Account statements'.

Inside, there are more folders labeled by the year.

Going back to 2018. I open 2023.

Inside, there are multiple Google Sheets arranged according to the month, starting from January.

I click open the sheet for January 2023 and start going through it.

Every sheet shows the credit, the debit, the source or beneficiary, and the remaining account balance. Over the next half an hour, I study every balance sheet closely.

There are many sources of income as well as expenditure, and I understand almost all of them.

But two debits occur regularly in every sheet which I have no idea about.

One is an NGO called Amara Charitable and the second is an account called Repair Department.

The reason I find the 'Repair Department' curious is because even though there are never huge transactions made to this account, there are multiple significant transactions over a period of time.

I start calculating the total amount debited to this department, and over a period of just three months, it crosses a few lakhs!

I don't understand. Was this how Mohan committed the financial fraud? By creating this fake account?

I go back and calculate the amount debited to Amara Charitable.

Same!

So someone has been using these fake accounts to embezzle funds.

Now whether it was really Hrehan or Mohan or someone entirely different, I have to find out.

XX

As I read the expenditure in April, another odd thing strikes me.

In this month, an expense that occurs regularly is 'food expenses'.

Now it would seem normal if we had a canteen that served all the office employees and we paid them a monthly amount.

But it is only in this month, and the amount is too extravagant to explain any monthly tea or meal bills.

And the weirdest thing is, in the data of the past six months, there have been no debits to Amara Charitable, Repair Department, or food expenses.

I minimize the Google Sheets window and open Google Chrome. I search for Amara Charitable.

There aren't many hits. But there are a few, and I click on the first hyperlink.

It's a website that declares that Amara Charitable is an NGO run with the help of government funding for the welfare of orphan girl children. The address shows somewhere in Pune.

There are a few pictures of random slum dwellers smiling at the camera, nothing more.

There is contact information given at the bottom. There is an email address and a contact number. I click a picture of the same.

And there is a 'Donate for our welfare' tab that takes me to account information.

I take down those details as well.

Next, I need to find out more about this Repair Department.

I minimize the search window and look at the desktop.

There are more folders.

I open a folder titled 'Important documents'.

There are a few files in this, all names marked in capital letters. I open the first one, titled 'Share document'.

This document is dated just one month before my accident.

As I carefully read, I realize that in this, I have been made the maximum shareholder in the shares held by the Malik group of industries. It is a legal document, notarized and signed by a lawyer and witnesses.

Yana had told me about this. She had said Hrehan had made me the maximum shareholder so that I would bear all the losses once the company went bankrupt after he had embezzled all the funds and eloped with money and his lover.

But something seems off. Something is odd.

I squint at the document and see the signatures again.

All the signatures are in blue ink, except Hrehan's. His is black.

Common sense tells me that if we all signed the document together, there is no reason why Hrehan alone would use a different ink.

I zoom in on his signature. I zoom out and zoom in on mine.

My suspicion is getting stronger by the minute.

After zooming in, my signature doesn't lose the continuity across pixels, but Hrehan's signature breaks up with each pixel.

Which confirms what I thought. His signature is a digital signature. Not actually signed by him.

But so what? Many documents are signed legally using a digital signature.

But the question remains.

Why would Hrehan sign such an important document using his digital signature?

I close the document and open the next, titled 'Nominee'.

This document dates two months before my accident.

This document shows that I have been made Hrehan's nominee in everything he owns.

I close my eyes, massaging my temples, elbows resting on the desktop desk. I try to remember what Yana had told me.

She had said Hrehan had made himself my nominee, and he was the one who orchestrated the accident, when his money laundering scheme failed, so that he could get my shares of the company after my demise.

But what I am seeing here is just the opposite.

I am the nominee to Hrehan's estate, in a legal document created just two months before the accident!

And as I scroll below, just as expected, all signatures are physically signed, except Hrehan's, which is digital.

My fingers tremble as I click the mouse to close this document.

My mind has started connecting the dots and I don't like where they are leading to.

There is a last unnamed file, which I click open, and Hrehan's digital signature stares me in the face, almost as if mocking me.

I close my eyes, trying to make sense of what I am seeing.

But I don't have time to lose.

I close the previous tabs, pushing all of my thoughts aside. I will have to deal with them later.

I go to Google Chrome and open my old email account. It is password protected, but now I know the password.

The last time I opened it, I had focused on Anaisha's e-mails.

Now I scroll through very carefully, checking every message that might seem random.

As I go months back, almost reaching the end of 2022, I see an e-mail.

'Congratulations. Your website has been successfully created' it announces.

There is some preamble which I skip, and rest my mouse on the link at the end below.

I swallow, brace myself, and click the mouse.

As I click the link, a web page appears.

I look at it in horror, as it is the webpage of Amara Charitable.

My entire body begins to tremble.

My breaths come fast as I hyperventilate.

Realization hits me in the gut.

I can't fathom what I have just uncovered.

It's not Hrehan. It's not Mohan. It's not Ronit. It's me! It has been me all along!

But before I can figure out what to do next, I feel something touching the back of my head.

Startled, I turn around, to come face to face with the barrel of a gun, which is now pointing bang in my face.

"R...Ronit?" I stutter, turning around in my chair as I come face to face with the man pointing the gun to my head.

He is the last person I expected to see here.

His face might be the same, but his expressions are different.

Instead of the usual soft expression, I see a cold face with a smirk.

Why does he want to kill me?

"Done with your research?" he asks, smiling a lop-sided smile, his neck tilting towards one side.

"What do you m-mean?" I ask, my survival instincts kicking in.

My hand tries to palpate behind me if I can find anything – a screwdriver, a paper-knife – anything that I can use as self-defense.

"Hands above your head, where I can see them," Ronit screams, kicking the chair next to him so that it turns and he gets seated in it, gun still pointed at my head.

I comply, placing my hands on my lap, my brain churning around to process what is going on.

"Where is the money?" he asks then.

"What money?" I ask, really clueless about what he is talking.

"Enough of your drama. You know what I am talking about," he screams, his face contorting with rage. "We have invested so much time and energy in you and this is what we get after waiting for one long year," he continues.

My mind focuses on the word 'We'. Who else is involved?

"I really have no idea what you are talking about," I try to say as calmly as my voice can allow.

Suddenly he stands up, training the barrel of the gun on my forehead.

He is so angry, I can feel his hand holding the gun trembling with rage.

"Transfer the money. NOW," he screams.

I close my eyes. Maybe this is how all of this ends.

And I will die never knowing what exactly happened.

"Ronit darling, don't do this. This will not get us anywhere."

A woman's voice interrupts us.

My eyes open wide with shock as I see Yana come and place one hand on Ronit's shoulder, pulling him back and making him sit down on the chair.

Ronit complies, but he still holds the gun pointed at me.

'Darling'??

Ronit and Yana are together?

"She really doesn't remember anything. We have to tell her what has happened till now. So that she can give us our money. And then we take care of the rest," she says to him, in a voice a mother uses to cajole a tantrum-throwing toddler.

Ronit sits there, still hyper-ventilating, gun pointed at my head, eyes locked with mine, and I feel pure terror coursing through my veins.

"Yana, how could you do this to me? You were my friend..." I begin.

"Oh, just shut up. You were a bitch before the accident. And you still are. And you deserve every bit of everything that is happening to you," she says, as she pulls another chair and sits down next to Ronit, facing me.

"I-I don't understand," I say.

I really don't.

What have I ever done to them? What have they been doing? Why are they doing this to me? Nothing makes sense at all!

"Do you remember Mrs Shamini Sethi?" Yana asks.

I try to scour the recesses of my mind. The name does sound familiar. It seems like the memory is there, somewhere, just out of my reach, but I can't quite reach it.

I shake my head.

Yana gives a hysterical laugh.

"Of course, you don't remember the woman you drove to suicide," she says.

What?

"What are you talking about?" I ask.

"She was my mother. One of the oldest employees of Malik Industries. She used to handle accounts before you married Hrehan. When you came, you wanted to fire her. Hrehan told you to have her as an assistant. Since she had been working for a long time, she would be able to guide you. But you wanted her gone. You wanted a monopoly over the accounts of Malik Industries. Because you had plans that my mom would never approve of. So you made a false allegation of stealth against her and got her fired. My mom pleaded, and begged you to not tarnish her reputation and career. But you didn't give a damn. Hrehan would, of course, believe his manipulative wife over his loyal, old employee because he is as much a wicked dog as you. But you didn't stop at just getting her fired. You withdrew her benefits. You saw to it that she could never get her provident fund, something she had saved since long from her salary for her retirement," Yana says in a harsh tone brimmed with emotions.

I swallow. This is hard enough to hear. And if this is true, I really must have been a very horrible person indeed.

"Of course, there was another reason why you wanted my mom gone. With the loose character that you have always had, you had already started having an illicit relationship with your best friend Ritu's husband who worked in the same department, and my mom, being the kind woman she is, tried to bring you back to your senses. But you thought she was blackmailing you and you just wanted her gone!"

I swallow hard.

"You know what my mom did then? When she not just lost the job she had given her entire life to, and her financial safety for her old age, but the respect she had earned over the course of her life? Well, difficult for you to understand though, how can you know what respect or reputation means?"

Yana laughs a dry laugh.

"She committed suicide".

A pin drop silence ensues. Hair on my arms and legs stand on end, and I feel terrible. I don't know what to say. How can I explain anything when I have no memory at all?

"So you see, that was when we decided to plot our revenge," Yana goes on.

"I am s-sorry for what happ-happened," I say.

"No, you are not," Ronit says, eyes boring into mine.

I look down. I can't look him in the eyes.

I don't know what they are going to reveal, but whatever it is, is not going to be good.

"Our biggest advantage was that you are a greedy woman with no morals," Yana continues.

"We dug into your life and found out everything about you, how you ditched your loyal boyfriend just for the sake of more money, a flashy lifestyle, and a rich husband, and how it drove him to suicide; how you left your father at the mercy of the hospice without ever bothering to check on him."

"Wait, what are you talking about? I used to visit my dad...," I start.

But Yana interrupts, smirking.

"Oh really? The last time you went to see him was sometime in 2017. You never went after that. And you want to know something else? Even after you hit the jackpot after getting Hrehan to get into a relationship with you, you tried to steal your father's pension money".

"I...what?" I ask, utterly dumbfounded.

"Yes. We spoke to your dad's lawyer. He has a restraining order against you. that prevents you from going to see your dad. They fear you might be after his life for the sake of his pension money".

I can't believe what she is saying.

"But guess what? They didn't need to take that restraining order against you. Because once it was crystal clear to you that you could no longer get any money from your father, you cut all ties with him. You never called, nor visited him. I would say he is a lucky man that he has Alzheimer's and doesn't have to realize what a monster his own daughter is."

I feel as if she is choking me, strangulating me with her words.

Was I really so bad? Am I?

Could I have tried to loot my own father's money?

My last memory of him is not very fond. We were never on the same page. And with his Alzheimers worsening, I had a hard time coping with him.

But, I loved my father, didn't I?

Hot tears fill my eyes, pricking them.

Yana continues, unaware of my internal turmoil.

"So, we knew that if we could take the right steps, making you fall into our trap was going to be a cake walk. We first tracked down your activities, your daily routine. And just immersed ourselves into it," Yana says, smiling a smile I can't begin to describe.

"W-What do you mean?" I ask. I still don't get it.

Supposedly, it was me who hired Ronit as the private investigator to look into Hrehan's affair.

Now, I have evidence that the affair was something completely orchestrated by me.

Then how does Ronit figure in all of this?

"Your crocodile tears are not going to help," Yana snaps.

It is then that I realize the hot tears that were pricking in my eyes are now flowing freely down. I have not had time to fathom what I just learnt about my father and what I have done.

I wipe the tears with the back of my hand.

"I met you at Yoga class. It was very easy to befriend you. You had no friends, thanks to your snobbish attitude and rude behaviour towards everyone in general. And since I tolerated all of your nonsense, I became your friend. Once we were friends, I introduced you to Ronit, as my dear brother," she laughs, pinching Ronit's cheek.

But Ronit doesn't smile or laugh, he just keeps his gun pointed at me with a straight face.

"As expected, it didn't take long for Ronit to seduce you. I didn't mind of course, because we were doing this for a good deed in the long term. And anyway, if you were ultimately going to die, why would it bother me at all?"

I feel a cold sensation running down my spine. Is this what they plan now? Killing me?

"So the first thing we did was to convince you that Ronit was your true love. Hrehan was working hard and hence found little time to pamper his high-maintenance wife. So that was what Ronit did. And soon you were swooped off your dirty feet by Ronit and his romantic gestures. Of course, as far as you were aware, I was not supposed to know about your clandestine little affair. But I did my bit by convincing you that Hrehan was failing as a husband in your marriage. In no time, we had you believe that Ronit was your soulmate like none other, and the thing you loved the most in the entire universe, money, could be yours and Ronit's," Yana says.

"How?" I ask.

"You worked in the Accounts department, and Ronit is a cyber expert. So we had access to the latest technology for conducting cyber fraud through Ronit and access to the company accounts through you. Even though I have always been the mastermind, you were never aware I was ever a part of any of this. You believed it was you and Ronit who planned the strategy."

I listen in rapt attention as she speaks.

"Of course, I did my part. I planted my source, my asset to work with you. Radha. She not only kept me updated about you and your whereabouts, but she also helped us bug your palace so that we were always aware of what you spoke with your husband. That was necessary for us to be sure that you were not double-crossing us, you know, knowing your loose ethics and morals."

"But then, Radha became greedy. She found out about what was happening between you and Ronit, thanks to her husband who dropped you when you went to meet Ronit, and they began blackmailing you."

"Anyway, coming back to the master plan. To begin with, we, as in you, started embezzling funds from company accounts. Ronit helped you set up a fake NGO, Amara Charitable. Whatever went to that account, went to a joint account opened by you and Ronit. But the account was opened using the dark web, through shell companies. Even if anyone tried, they wouldn't be able to figure out where the money went," Yana says.

This is not news to me. Just before Ronit stuck the barrel of the gun into the backside of my head, I had discovered that Amara Charitable's website had been created by me. And it was very clear what my intentions would have been.

"We created another similar account, the Repair Department. If traced, it showed that the money was going to the account of the Repair Department of Malik Industries. But it was actually being diverted to another off-shore account. Again, don't ask me how. Thanks to our cyber and dark web expert," Yana says, indicating Ronit.

I look over at Ronit and his cold gaze doesn't even flinch.

"But the entire credit, of course, goes to you. You see, without you, we wouldn't have been able to pull this off. You slowly and steadily stole money from the company, without a soul suspecting anything. And I must applaud you. This system worked fine for months together," Yana says, clapping her hands slowly.

"What about the food expenses for April? What were those?" I ask.

"That? Well, that was a short detour. Now you see, we couldn't just keep stealing money from the company forever. There had to be a limit. Once we had sufficient balance, we decided to get rid of Hrehan," she says.

I shudder.

What??

Was *I* really a part of the *we*?

"Well, at least that was what you believed. Our plan was a bit more than that. It was to get rid of Hrehan first, and then you, so that me and Ronit could take all the money and go to a faraway land, to live our perfect fairy tale".

And they laugh together heartily. I look at them, laughing like maniacs, as a chill runs down my spine.

I know they are a selfish and crooked pair, but I can't stop thinking about how cruel, selfish, insensitive, and mean I have been before the accident! How could I have been such a prude?

I was plotting the murder of my unsuspecting husband with my lover, and planning to rob him before doing that!

Who even does that?

Yana is probably right. I deserve this. Karma is getting back at me!

More hot tears roll down my cheeks as I wait for Yana to stop laughing maniacally and tell me more.

"So, coming back to our original plan. Our first plan was to get rid of Hrehan from the company. We didn't plan to murder him right away, no. We are not that evil," she laughs as if that is funny.

I ignore her laughter but listen in rapt attention.

"We planned to tarnish his image, and maybe, send him to jail so that you could become the owner of Malik Industries by proxy and thus gain complete control over all the money and estate. That was why we planted Anaisha as Hrehan's secretary. You picked a girl from a nightclub who said she was willing to do any job if someone paid the right amount of money, and made her Hrehan's secretary."

"Her job was to try and lure Hrehan into her trap, seduce him and collect evidence, and then file a case of molestation and sexual harassment against him. Simultaneously, you also made her your accomplice in acquiring confidential and classified information regarding the company's affairs from Hrehan's computer. Sometimes, she would get those files for you on a pen drive, and sometimes, she signaled for you whenever his cabin was empty, so that you could go and check his computer for the latest dealings and updates. This helped us stay two steps ahead in our financial transactions. She also took care of CCTV footage so that no such evidence was left."

I remember the flashback I had where I was sitting at Hrehan's desk in his office. Was this what I had been doing then?

"Unfortunately, even though Anaisha proved to be an asset when it came to accessing information from Hrehan's laptop, she proved useless for the main work we hired her for. She could not prove her charges of sexual harassment efficiently and finally, it was she who got fired after the internal inquiry. Yet, to keep her mouth shut, we had to pay her off. That is what is the 'food expenses for April'," Yana says.

Now dots are beginning to connect, and I can see the picture becoming clearer by the minute.

"Now since we could not get rid of Hrehan from the company, we decided to get rid of him from the universe. But before we could do that, we needed to be sure you would be the beneficiary if something happened to him," Yana goes on, apparently enjoying this little storytelling stint.

"Initially, you tried to weave your magic around Hrehan so that he would make you a shareholder in his company. Till then, you were nothing but an employee of the Malik group of industries. But of course, Hrehan is an intelligent businessman. He would never mix profession with pleasure. So just to appease you, he made you a 5% shareholder in the company."

"I remember how angry you were that day. We had a wild time that night," Ronit says, smiling sadistically, speaking for the first time in a long while.

I cringe at the thought and shake the images of what he just said forming inside my head. Yana laughs too. "That was when Ronit came to our rescue once more. We created fake documents, which not even the best attorney in the world could refute. The first document was the one where Hrehan has made you the maximum stakeholder in his company."

So it is true that I was made the maximum stakeholder in the company. But not by Hrehan, for me to bear the maximum losses when it went bankrupt as Yana had previously told me. It was a forged document!

"But the lawyer's signature?" I question, as even though Hrehan's signature seemed digital, the lawyer's signature looked real, and he was our company's lawyer.

"Again, thanks to Ronit and some cyber technology. We got AI to create exact replicas of the lawyer's signature based on his signatures in other documents in the company. The documents that YOU provided us," Yana smiles.

"We also needed to get everything in your name once Hrehan died. So we created the nominee certificate which again is fake, but legally signed by your lawyer as well as Hrehan," Yana smiles.

"You just don't know about the third document, because it doesn't exist on your desktop. The document that transfers all of your belongings, property, money, and estate to the owner and co-founder of Amara Charitable, Mr. Ronit Sharma, after you die," she continues smiling wickedly, her hands gesturing towards Ronit as if handing him some imaginary award.

"So you want to kill me now so that you can be the owner of everything?" I ask bitterly.

"Are you an idiot? If that was so, I wouldn't be explaining all of this to you, you dimwit woman. I would have directly killed you," Yana screams, suddenly losing all the composure of moments ago. She probably suffers from bipolar psychosis.

"You have ruined all of our plans," she says with gritted teeth.

Their plans included murdering me and stealing Hrehan's property. So whatever might have been my role in all of this, I am still happy that it fizzled out.

Yet I cannot fathom how evil I was to plan all of this with them! And without even realizing that they were two-timing me! Backstabbing me!

"It was the day of your birthday – our D-day. We hired a contract killer – Rupesh - who would mow down your husband in a hit-and-run and then disappear off the face of the earth along with his vehicle – a vehicle which would have a fake number plate that would be removed immediately after the accident and the vehicle would be painted overnight so that no CCTV camera would ever pick up where it went. You paid the man half the money in cash, the day before and told him what he had to do. You promised to pay the remaining amount once the job was done."

"You then insisted that Hrehan hold a small party for your birthday and invite your office colleagues, as you had no friends anyway. You would party till way past midnight. And then, when the roads were empty and it was dark, you would lure Hrehan to the intersection of roads in front of City Mall where Rupesh would drive the speeding truck into him."

"Rupesh asked how he would identify Hrehan, as he had never seen him. You showed him a photo, but obviously that wouldn't help much considering it would be midnight and dark. So you told him that Hrehan would be wearing a grey coat. You said you would make sure he wore that to your party," Yana says, her voice escalating in tone and speed as she says this.

And suddenly the world spins around me.

I am no longer in the office, gun trained at my head, at the mercy of Yana and Ronit, listening to the sordid tale of our evil conspiracy.

Instead, I am walking on a road, laughing hard, my head spinning from far too many drinks. It's dark and the roads are deserted.

"Wait, Mihika, stop. You are drunk," Hrehan calls from behind me.

But I don't stop. I keep walking.

I am ecstatic. It is my birthday celebration, and I don't know about others but I have enjoyed it like anything. I had a peg too many and I danced like a peacock on the dance floor. Now the world is spinning around me and...

Suddenly, I feel one of the thin strips of the silk dress I am wearing snap across my left shoulder, and the strap of the dress on my left chest suddenly hangs loose, exposing me. Suddenly conscious despite the drinks and my fizzled brain, I let out a small shriek.

Hrehan runs to catch up with me. He notices what has happened, as I attempt to cover myself with my arms crossed in front of me, fighting to maintain balance on my wriggly feet.

"Wait. Don't worry. Wear this," Hrehan says, removing his grey coat, and putting it around my shoulders, covering me.

He wraps his arm around me and says, "Come, let's hail a taxi and head home".

My brain has stopped processing anything and I just follow what he says.

And we walk to the intersection in front of the city Mall.

A few steps.

A flash of light.

A loud screech of brakes.

A horrible, ear-shattering horn.

Something hits me hard.
And everything goes blank.

Someone slaps me hard across my face. I am startled as water is sprinkled harshly across it.

I open my eyes and look around, my brain reeling from the momentary confusion.

I am still sitting in the chair I was in, Yana and Ronit staring at me.

"She's awake," he tells her.

"I wore the coat that night," I say, my voice sounding like a croaking frog with my parched throat.

"What?" they ask in unison.

"I was wearing Hrehan's grey coat. That was probably why he hit me instead of Hrehan," I explain.

Now I know what happened.

And that explains why this guy, Rupesh, has been following me in his red car.

I never paid him the rest of the money!

"Yes, we know. That was the dumbest thing for even a dumb woman like you," Yana says with disdain. "Rupesh was after us for the money while you lay in the hospital, in a coma. Finally, we told him to go after you when you woke up. You owed him money, not us," Yana says.

I nod. Now everything makes sense.

I know what I did.

I hatched a plan to loot my husband and get him murdered, steal his property and estate, and elope with my lover and all the money.

I didn't know that I was just a pawn in this entire scheme right from the beginning, and my fate would soon match Hrehan's if he died.

But what doesn't make any sense is, what is the intention of these two now?

Why are these two holding me captive here?

Why did they come back into my life with planned and organized lies?

Why are they even telling me everything that happened?

They prompted me to come to the office tonight and access my computer. Why are they doing this?

Which money have they been talking about?

And most important of all, why have they not killed me yet?

"What do you want from me?" I ask.

"Our money. All the money that we saved," Yana says coldly.

I decide, enough is enough.

"I don't remember any of the things you are telling me. And I may have been your partner in crime when all of this happened, even if for you two, I was just the next victim. For me, all of this has happened a lifetime ago. The accident has changed me. It has changed the way I think. It has changed the way I behave. If given a chance to go back and undo things, I would. But all I can do now is tell you I don't want to be a part of this. And you are not escaping either. I don't care if I go to prison too for being a co-conspirator. I am going to come clean to Hrehan and the police. I will no longer be a part of your ....".

"Shut up," Ronit screams, pointing the gun at my head again. "What do you think we have come here for? Penance?"

Yana laughs like a horse.

"We want what belongs to us. And then, you can only come clean to the police and Hrehan if you live. Which you won't," Ronit says thrusting the gun against my forehead, making a point.

"I don't have any money. You both have it, from the accounts of Amara Charitable and Repair Department," I speak up in revolt.

"No, they don't," a voice says from the door, and we turn around to look at the person who said this.

It's a police officer in uniform, and he has a gun in his hand, pointed at Ronit.

"You called the police?" Yana asks me, looking wildly around as more police officers surround us, all guns trained at Yana and Ronit.

I don't reply.

Yana and Ronit are still looking at the police officers surrounding us, completely bewildered.

"Surrender your weapon," the inspector tells Ronit.

Ronit looks at Yana like a lost child, unsure of what to do. At that moment, I realize that Yana is the mastermind behind all of this. Ronit is also just a puppet in her hands who dances to her tunes.

And a thought strikes me. Was she ever really, truly in love with Ronit, or was he too just a pawn like me, a target to be finished off once the job was done? We will probably never know!

She nods at him sternly, and Ronit complies. They both raise their hands.

Two police officers then proceed to put handcuffs around Ronit and Yana's wrists as Yana keeps blabbering to Ronit that he shouldn't worry and that she knows the best lawyers who will get them out in a jiffy.

As the pair is escorted to police vehicles, the inspector comes to me and introduces himself.

"Hello. I am Inspector Ashwin," he says. I remember hearing his name from Hrehan as the police inspector in charge of my case.

I have lots of questions for him, but my body and mind feel frozen as I haven't recovered from the shock of what just happened.

"Did they hurt you?" he asks. "We are going to take you to a hospital to get you checked up," he says.

I don't understand.

"Aren't you arresting me?" I ask.

"No," comes a voice from behind Inspector Ashwin.

It's Hrehan. Oh my God! How much does he know?

When my eyes meet his, my eyes well up with tears.

I feel so bad for what I have put him through.

"I...I am...Sorr-sorry..." I begin but my throat feels choked up with emotions.

Hrehan places a hand on my shoulder.

"It's okay. It's over," he says.

I feel overwhelmed with emotions again. The view across my eyes blurs as my corneas get covered with a fresh film of thick tears.

"Can we have a moment alone please?" Hrehan asks Inspector Ashwin as sobs escape my body, gently rocking my frame.

"She needs a medical check-up," Ashwin says.

"I will bring her to the hospital," Hrehan assures Inspector Ashwin.

After the police depart, Hrehan pulls a chair and sits across me.

I let out my feelings of anger and frustration – anger with myself and frustration over what I have done – as tears flow down my cheeks like a tap let loose.

Hrehan just sits, patting my back, consoling me.

He doesn't deserve me.

"You know...everything?" I ask finally when my sobs have settled down.

"Yes," he says in a pensive voice.

"Since when? Why didn't you do anything? And what happened to the money? How did you know I was here? How did the police reach here just in time?" I ask, hundreds of questions swarming my brain as I try to grapple with reality.

Hrehan takes a deep breath and clears his throat. I brace myself for what he has to tell me.

"I knew nothing about what was going on till your accident. I had no idea what was happening in your life and what you were doing behind my back. Once you landed in the hospital, I had to take charge of your work here till I could find a replacement. It was then that I realized that funds were being embezzled from the company accounts."

"Is that why you fired Mohan?" I ask.

"How do you know about Mohan?" Hrehan questions.

I shrug.

"No. I fired him because I got to know about your affair with him," he says.

"Oh," I reply.

"How did you come to know?"

"I...I went through your chats on your mobile when you were in the hospital," Hrehan says.

I swallow. Going through my mobile while I was in a coma might be wrong, but it is nothing compared to the crimes I have committed.

"Didn't you know about it when I broke my friendship with the girls?"

"No. You never told me what happened. Nor did Ritu. So I had no idea," Hrehan says.

"Does that mean I was still having an affair with Mohan till I met with an accident?" I ask, feeling my face burn with shame. Because I know I was also in a relationship with Ronit at the time.

"Probably. The messages were definitely too intimate for colleagues. And when I confronted Mohan with those messages, he confessed. He did say you were no longer together, but I didn't want that bastard in my company anymore," Hrehan says.

He goes on when I don't say anything.

"That is how I realized you were also having an affair with Ronit, and planning certain things with him. Of course, you guys were not naïve to leave proof of any such conversation on your cell phone. But I suspected you were up to something, and I hired a dark web guy who recovered deleted messages and emails from your cellphone, and I got a hint of what you had been planning with Ronit. At the same time, I learned about the money being transferred to dicey accounts that could not be traced. But the guy I hired is an expert in that field, and he helped me track down the offshore accounts under the fake names of Amara Charitable and Repair Department. It took him some time but he finally did get the access. Then I used your mobile to access those accounts and withdrew all the money that had been shuttled from the company."

I listen in rapt attention.

So Hrehan had quickly uncovered my plans. How did he salvage the situation?

Hrehan takes another deep breath before going on.

"I conducted an internal audit of the accounts department and created two separate funds to show that this money was being used there as a safe keep for the company's expenses, so that the money, which amounted to crores, could be shunted back to the company, slowly, step by step, without raising any red flags with the ED. The funds are now slowly being transferred back, piece by piece."

That explains what Ronit and Yana were trying to do.

After all their planning and scheming, I ended up in a coma and they lost the money we had stolen till then. That is why they were desperate for me to come to the office so that they could make me transfer the money back to them, and then they could kill me. That is also the reason why both tried to make me believe that Hrehan was an abusive husband so that I would believe both of them and do as they said. But they had no idea that I was also just as clueless about where that money went as they were.

We sit in silence for some time.

"Why didn't you leave me?" I ask Hrehan then.

Because if I came to know that my spouse had plotted with their lover to murder me, I would definitely leave them.

Hrehan really doesn't deserve a woman like me.

"To tell you the truth, I was indeed very angry and hurt when I learnt about all of this. But I couldn't leave you while you were in a coma. And when you woke up, you had no memory of anything that had happened. I thought that probably it was a blessing in disguise. I decided to give you, and us, another chance. And somehow, from the time you have woken up, you seem changed. Your behaviour has changed, you seem like a different person. A better version of yourself," Hrehan says.

"That doesn't make any of the crimes committed by me any less real," I say as more tears now flow down my cheeks.

"Aren't you going to report me to the police?" I ask, my voice now groggy from the tears.

"For what? For plotting to kill me? You just made the plan, never acted on it, right?"

"No, I acted on it, don't you realize?" I ask.

Hrehan looks at me, confused.

"The man that hit me in that hit-and-run was supposed to mow you down. He hit me because I was wearing your coat," I cry.

Hrehan looks perplexed for a few moments as he fathoms what I just said.

"How do you know you were wearing my coat?" he asks.

I shake my head.

"I get flashbacks. I see some things that resurface from my memory. They happen at random times, at random places. I don't know what might trigger a flashback. This was one of the many flashbacks I have had since," I say.

We both sit in heavy silence for some time.

"How did the police turn up here just in time?" I ask, still puzzled about how all of this happened.

Hrehan clears his throat again.

"From the time you woke up, I knew the guy you were planning everything with would try to contact you, he would be desperate to get his hands on the stolen money that had vanished from your accounts. So I had bugged your phone. I had bugged our home and car. I kept a watch on everything you did, every person you met, every conversation you had. Because that was the only way I could save us from these people. Today, I had Inspector

Ashwin in the loop right from the beginning. When we realized what was happening, he immediately responded by bringing over his team to arrest those two. We have recorded your entire conversation, just in case."

I nod in understanding.

"So you knew about those fake legal documents?" I ask.

"No. I never suspected anything of that sort, and hence I never explored your desktop for anything more other than account statements. I got to know about it now, when Yana told you, as I was listening to everything," he says.

"You should file a complaint against me. For embezzlement of company funds," I say.

"Which funds? What embezzlement?" Hrehan smiles.

I laugh a dry, throaty laugh.

"Did I really ever love you?" I ask, shaking my head.

"I believe you did," Hrehan says, and I can see his eyes turning moist.

"You really don't deserve me," I say, as more tears cascade down my cheeks.

"I probably didn't deserve the old you, but I definitely deserve the new you," Hrehan says, holding my hands in his, and we sob together for a long time.

EPILOGUE 1

Three days later

I am sitting across from my neurologist, Dr Paresh.

I am trying to understand why I am a changed person after the coma, why I can't identify with the person I was before the accident.

"You know, our brain is really very mysterious. But many things, including how we behave, speak, think, and feel, depend on the proper functioning of areas of the brain designated for that purpose," the doctor says.

"You mean, the traumatic brain injury I suffered changed me? My thinking?" I ask.

"Yes, that is the only possibility I can think of. The behavioural patterns and emotions we feel are controlled by the prefrontal cortex, a part of your brain that lies on the very front side, just behind your forehead. There is also a small almond-shaped structure in the brain called the Amygdala that controls your deepest emotions. Now you were in a coma because of a brain injury. You slowly recovered from it and gained consciousness. But not all pathological processes reverse within six months, right? So there might be a small inflammation or bleeding in these structures that has distorted their neural connections. And neural connections, once broken, can form new connections. Think of it in terms of electricity lines. One line fuses, you create another line, an alternate pathway, to conduct the electricity, right?"

I nod, beginning to understand what he is trying to say.

"Many people experience behavioural changes for months after their traumatic brain injury. You know, there have also been some interesting cases in which people waking after a coma have started speaking an entirely foreign language or in an entirely different accent!" he tells me.

I nod.

"So what is the possibility that I will revert to being the same person I was before? Start thinking the same way as before?" I ask the main question I came here to ask. Because I don't want to become that person. I hate her!

"Nobody can really predict that. But if you like the new person you are right now, let's hope you stay as you are," he says.

Outside the hospital, I look up at the sunlit sky interspersed with cottony white clouds, I look around at the hustle and bustle of the city running around me, the leaves of trees swaying silently in the breeze, the cafe across the street teeming with people laughing and chatting with each other as they go about just another day in their lives.

It makes me realize that I have always taken everything in life for granted.

And everything was almost taken away from me. Because of my karma.

But the universe has given me a second chance.

Life has granted me a second chance to rewrite the remaining blank pages of my life.

And how I write them is entirely up to me.

So I close my eyes. I make a vow to myself.

I will make the rest of my life, the best of my life!

EPILOGUE 2

Eight months later

It's been eight months since the rendezvous with Yana and Ronit.

I still have very little memory of the past six years of my life.

But I am happy this way. I don't want any reminders of what kind of woman I had turned into or what kind of crimes I had been committing.

I have decided not to go for any more hypnotherapy sessions with Dr.Veeksha despite her suggestion that I should continue. I don't want the shadow of my past life on this new life that I have decided to build for myself.

I thank God for everything he has given me and for the life I have ahead.

Hrehan is just the same loving and caring husband he has been since I can remember, but now I don't doubt him. I trust him more than myself. I still think I deserved some punishment for what I did, but Hrehan refuses to file any police complaint.

The man who had been after me for money, the contract killer Rupesh, has also been caught, with inputs from Yana and Ronit, and all three of them will be in jail for a long time.

I went to Pune two months back as I still needed to make things right. I met Ritika, and it took some time and convincing, but finally, she agreed to meet me, and I got the chance to apologize to her, and let her know that I terribly repented what the past me had done. I met Nikhil's parents too, and even though they weren't exactly as forgiving as Ritika, I still felt like I got my redemption by meeting them.

Next, I met the lawyer who had put the restraining order against me meeting my dad. I convinced him that I had absolutely no ill intentions, despite whatever had happened in the past, and that I just wanted to meet my dad. Hrehan helped me convince the lawyer, as the lawyer was very skeptical about my intentions, and I couldn't blame him, given my history. He took a notarized written undertaking from me that I would not try to steal from my father again, and I was more than happy to give it.

When I met my dad, it was an overwhelming experience. For just a tiny moment, when he looked at me, he squeezed his eyes, and I almost thought he recognized me. Well, almost. Then he asked me who I was. But that has not deterred me. He is still my father and I love him. I will love him till my very last breath.

So I have started visiting him every weekend. Every weekend I make the trip from Mumbai to Pune and back. I spend the entire day with him. We eat together, I help him with his gardening activities, something he spends hours doing. I read to him, we watch movies. And this time that I spend with him, is the best time ever!

I met Ritu last month. Of course, she didn't want to see my face, and understandably so. But Hrehan spoke to her, and she convinced her to give me a chance. She has already separated from Mohan, and I am the person to blame for it. I sincerely apologized to her. It has taken time and effort from my side, but she is slowly warming up to me, forgiving me, and I hope our friendship rekindles without a shadow of the past.

For obvious reasons, I have no interest in meeting Shanaya and Koel. I don't want such people in my life. But I am in touch with Ayesha and she has become a good friend over the past months. I have joined our office back as an accountant, and I have been working really hard to do everything right and keep transparency in all accounts. I deleted all the fake legal documents I had created with the help of Ronit and Yana.

Despite my protests, Hrehan has made me a 25% shareholder in the company. I insisted he shouldn't. I am no longer interested in material things. I just want to be happy and satisfied with what I have. Because I have realized that these are the only two things that actually matter.

Coming back to Hrehan, we don't sleep separately anymore. I am more than happy to be with him, in every moment, and I have learnt to treasure what I have the hard way.

I am never going to lose that, ever.

EPILOGUE 3

Two years later

Today I joined a gym, as I need to keep myself physically fit as well as mentally sound.

As I try lifting the various weights, I feel a hand on my shoulder.

I turn around.

"New to weight training?" a heavy masculine voice asks.

I look at the man addressing me.

He is tall, dusky, muscular, and masculine in a very attractive way. His ripped biceps threaten to tear the sleeves of his tee shirt and I start feeling butterflies in my stomach. His chiseled, clean-shaved jaw makes me go slightly weak in my knees. His track pants...

"Are you done checking me out?" he smiles a lop-sided smile and I am suddenly aware that I have been staring him up and down.

I blush, and smile, biting my lower lip with my teeth.

If this handsome guy is going to train me, I wouldn't mind coming here daily, right?

And a little flirting won't harm, would it?

THE END

About The Author

Dr Ketaki Patwardhan Nirkhi

Dr. Ketaki Patwardhan Nirkhi, is an Anaesthetist by profession and a writer by passion.

Her debut novel, 'Those Enchanted Four and Half Years,' was a love story set against the backdrop of events occurring in a medical college, published by Rainbow Publishers. Her short stories and poems have been published in ezines like Indus Woman Writing, Short Story Book, Blogger Park, Creative Writing, Poetry Craze, Momspresso, and Writers Café.

Psychological and suspense thrillers is her genre and she has published many such thrillers, namely, The Missing Connection, The Long Lost Path, Hello Stranger– the man behind the mask, The dangerous game, The mysterious neighbour, The Girl with no name, A Rose amongst thorns, The Blue Envelope, The Canvas, S.T.A.L.K.E.D, The Destination Wedding, The Labyrinth, Anonymous, The life of Myra, The Vixen, Unbelievable and Finding Kavya.

She stays in Thane with her husband and a daughter who inherits her mother's writing genes.

www.ingramcontent.com/pod-product-compliance
Lightning Source LLC
LaVergne TN
LVHW041213150826
845673LV00001B/388

* 9 7 9 8 8 9 6 9 9 6 9 4 1 *